Samuel French Acting Edition

I0584690

Anne of Green Gables

by Alice Chadwicke

Adapted from
L.M. Montgomery's novel

ISBN 978-0-573-60542-0

www.concordtheatricals.com
www.concordtheatricals.co.uk

Please refer to page 135 for further copyright information.

ANNE OF GREEN GABLES

STORY OF THE PLAY

Mark Twain, the celebrated humorist, was so taken with the quaint charm of L. M. Montgomery's tremendously popular novel that upon reading it for the first time he literally rushed to endorse it. "In 'Anne of Green Gables' you will find the dearest and most moving and delightful girl since the immortal Alice." And for years this fascinating book has headed the list of best sellers. It has been printed and reprinted, has been made twice as a movie, once as a silent picture and only recently as a talkie, but it has remained for the distinguished dramatist, Alice Chadwicke, to make the first and only dramatization of this magically beautiful story. Green Gables is the home of lovable Matthew Cuthbert and his stern sister, Marilla Cuthbert. Marilla has never been known to thaw out. Nobody suspects that beneath her hard exterior there lurks a soft and tender heart. When Matthew, after a great deal of reflection, finally decides to adopt an orphan boy to help with his farm work, Marilla grudgingly consents. Through a rattlebrained friend of theirs, one Nancy Spencer, they agree to take a boy from The Hopeton Orphanage. Marilla makes ready to receive the boy and Matthew drives to the station to get him. Fancy his consternation when he finds little Anne Shirley waiting for him! There has been a mistake and Anne has been sent to Green Gables in lieu of the boy whom the Cuthberts plan to adopt. There is nothing else to do but to take Anne home and let her stay, at least over night. But from the instant Anne and Matthew meet a strong attachment grows up between the little orphan and the man who has been starving for affection without realizing it. Anne, with her vivid imagination, her charitable viewpoint, her refreshing simplicity, touches the old bachelor's heart. But not so with Marilla. She determines to send Anne back to the orphanage the following day. But she reckons without Anne, who is so enchanted by everything at Green Gables and who cries and begs and pleads so hard to remain that even Marilla, "just to please Matthew, of course," finally gives in and consents. The comedy that ensues through Anne's many unfortunate mistakes caused by her all too vivid imagination, her loyalty to Matthew and Marilla, her attachment for her bosom friend, Diana Barry, her feud with Gilbert Blythe, the wealthiest boy in town, the episode of Marilla's old amethyst brooch and many more heart-warming incidents are finely woven into this play. Anne is the sort of part that every young girl will adore playing, and the other parts offer splendid opportunities to the various members of the cast. Marilla is a great part for a character actress, as is Mrs. Rachel Lynde, who lives on the adjoining farm. Then there is young Josie Pye, a lad named Moody Spurgeon and, among the many others, Matthew Cuthbert, Anne's kindred spirit. The play breathes of youth, is thoroughly modern in spirit, very simple to prepare and present and Miss Chadwicke has written into it such an abundance of warmth, wit and motion that it becomes an endless delight. "Anne of Green Gables" will pack your theatres to their capacity, and your audiences will request you to repeat it again and again. It is entirely different from any play you have ever selected, and one that will bring added laurels to each and every group fortunate enough to secure it.

TO

L. M. MONTGOMERY,

who created the most lovable heroine
the world of fiction has ever known,
this play is most earnestly dedicated.
ALICE CHADWICKE.

CAST OF CHARACTERS

ANNE SHIRLEY, *an orphan, our adorable young heroine.*

FLORENCE REMSEN, *Superintendent of The Hopeton Orphanage.*

MINNIE STEARN, *an attendant at the orphanage.*

MRS. ALEXANDER SPENCER, *who has a difficult time talking.*

MATTHEW CUTHBERT, *Anne's champion and a "kindred spirit."*

MARILLA CUTHBERT, *his sister, who refuses to thaw out.*

MRS. RACHEL LYNDE, *who loves to give advice.*

MRS. BARRY, *a wealthy matron.*

DIANA BARRY, *her daughter, who becomes Anne's bosom friend.*

MRS. ALLAN, *the new Minister's charming wife.*

JOSIE PYE, *in Anne's class at school.*

MOODY SPURGEON, *another schoolmate.*

GILBERT BLYTHE, *the wealthiest boy in town.*

IRA MILLS, *a wealthy business man.*

SYNOPSIS OF SCENES

ACT ONE

SCENE I: *The reception room of The Hopeton Orphan Asylum. Noon of a day in early summer.*

SCENE II: *The sitting room of the Cuthberts' home at Green Gables, Avonlea. Late afternoon of the following day.*

ACT TWO

The same.   The following September; afternoon.

ACT THREE

SCENE I: *The same. Two years later; an afternoon in April.*
SCENE II: *The same. Two months later; an evening in June.*

TIME: *The present.*

DESCRIPTION OF CHARACTERS

FLORENCE REMSEN: *A tall, imposing appearing woman in her early forties. She is the Superintendent of the asylum. Wears a stiffly starched white uniform, the sort that a graduate nurse affects; no cap. Her shoes and stockings are also white. She is immaculately groomed and gives the impression of being highly efficient. Although she is strict about having her orders obeyed, she is, by nature, kindly and benevolent.*

MINNIE STEARN: *She is all that her name implies; possessed of a forbidding aspect, she is most unpleasant in manner, intolerant in her viewpoint and is inclined to be irritated by the slightest happening. Thirty-eight years of age, she is tall and thin—the typical old maid. Wears a severely plain dress of blue gingham, the sort that an undergraduate nurse would wear. Black shoes. Horn-rimmed glasses add to her dour appearance.*

ANNE SHIRLEY *is in her middle teens, but because of her frail build and slight stature, she may be played by an older girl who possesses all of the attributes of extreme youth. Then, too, make up and youthful dress cause her to appear extremely juvenile. Grave and solemn in manner, there is about her an aura of elfish charm, a whimsical something that completely envelops her. Life is terribly serious to ANNE SHIRLEY, a fact that causes her to draw heavily*

9

upon her imagination. She must be played with utter simplicity. The more natural she is the more her audiences will love her and take her to their hearts. Her hair is parted in the center and hangs down her back in two long braids. There are several freckles on her nose and a disturbing few on other parts of her face.

MRS. ALEXANDER SPENCER: *A short, stout woman in her early fifties. She is obviously a small town housewife with a kind heart and a desire to help others. She is dressed in a coat suit that has long since been outmoded, a hat with a few colored flowers on it; carries a purse and an umbrella.*

MARILLA CUTHBERT: *A tall, well-built woman in her late forties. She is a woman of rigid conscience who has her own ideas as to the fitness of things. Her hair is streaked with grey and is gathered in a small knot at the back with a few wire hairpins to hold the knot in place. MARILLA is always neat and tidy, but there is never an attempt at ostentation. Her gingham housedress is made along conventional lines. Her black shoes are of the buttoned type. She has her knitting and knitting needles in her hand. Beneath her stern exterior there is a human quality lurking and trying to make itself evident, but MARILLA spends her life trying to hide this from the world. Her real nature is masked by a gruffness, a strictness that is difficult to penetrate.*

MRS. MILDRED BARRY: *A fine-appearing woman in her late forties. She is cultured and refined in manner, possessed of a lovely smile and a frank and sincere nature.*

MRS. RACHEL LYNDE: *A tall, thin, angular woman of uncertain years. She is the village busybody* and is never so happy as when prying into other people's affairs.

MATTHEW CUTHBERT: *He is a short man in his late fifties. The top of his head is entirely bald and the remaining fringe of hair on the sides is pure white. Generous, charitable, benevolent, his kindly nature is reflected in his face. The world would be an easier place to live in if there were more Matthews. Diffident and shy, he has seldom dared to venture an opinion and has been completely under* MARILLA'S *dominance.*

JOSIE PYE: *A tall, gangling girl of fifteen. She is at that awkward age when she appears to be even gawkier than she really is. She giggles constantly and tries to assume a most superior manner. She is at her best when relating a choice piece of gossip. Her hair hangs in one long braid down her back and is tied with a ribbon.*

GILBERT BLYTHE: *A manly and fine-looking boy of about sixteen.* GILBERT *is possessed of an extremely attractive personality, and in spite of the fact that he is all boy and enjoys playing pranks, he is sincere and refined in manner, intelligent and of good breeding.*

DIANA BARRY: *A pretty girl about the same age as* ANNE. *She, too, may be played by an older girl who looks younger because of her small size.* DIANA *is inclined to be plump. She is of an affectionate nature, earnest and sincere, but lacks* ANNE'S *great imagination.*

MOODY SPURGEON: *A tall, awkward appearing boy of fifteen.* MOODY *has a permanent expression of sadness on his face and never has been known to smile.*

MRS. ALLAN: *A gracious and charming woman in her early thirties. She has a ready smile and a fine understanding of humanity.*

IRA MILLS *is a tall, powerfully built man in his early fifties, pompous and distinguished in appearance.*

Anne Of Green Gables

ACT ONE

SCENE I

SCENE: *The reception room of The Hopeton Orphan Asylum.*

TIME: *Noon of a day in early summer.*

SET: *Just a small corner of the room is shown, so that it may be set inside the big set that stands for the rest of the play. The inset consists of a couple of plain wings with a door over Right with interior backing. A small wooden bench and a table with three straight-backed chairs surrounding it is all the furniture that is necessary.*

AT RISE OF CURTAIN: FLORENCE REMSEN, *a tall, imposing appearing woman in her early forties, sits in chair behind table. She is the Superintendent of the asylum. Wears a stiffly starched white uniform, the sort that a graduate nurse affects; no cap. Her shoes and stockings are also white. She is immaculately groomed and gives the impression of being highly efficient. Although she is strict about having her orders obeyed, she is, by nature, kindly and benevolent. The instant the Curtain rises,* FLORENCE *crosses to door* R.

FLORENCE. *(Calling off* R. *loudly)* Miss Minnie! Oh, Miss Minnie! What is delaying you?

MINNIE. *(Off stage* R. ; *nervously)* I'm here, Miss Remsen. I'll be right in.

(FLORENCE *retraces her steps to behind table and resumes her seat in chair.* MINNIE STEARN *enters* R., *carrying a few letters in her hand. She is all that her name implies; possessed of a forbidding aspect, she is most unpleasant in manner, intolerant in her viewpoint and is inclined to be irritated by the slightest happening. Thirty-eight years of age, she is tall and thin— the typical old maid. Wears a severely plain dress of blue gingham, the sort that an undergraduate nurse would wear. Black shoes. Horn-rimmed glasses add to her dour appearance.)*

FLORENCE. *(Looking at* MINNIE *as the latter enters)* Oh, you've brought the mail, I see.

MINNIE. *(Comes to* R. *of table, handing the letters to* FLORENCE; *complainingly)* I'm so terribly upset it's a wonder I remembered to think of the mail. Anybody else in my position wouldn't have.

FLORENCE. *(Inspecting the letters)* Why, what's the matter now?

MINNIE. *(Savagely)* The same thing that's always the matter. It's that Anne.

FLORENCE. *(Opening one of the letters and removing same from envelope)* You mean Anne Shirley? (MINNIE *nods angrily.)* Why, what has she done now?

MINNIE. *(Angrily)* You mean what hasn't she done. I haven't had one peaceful day since that girl was admitted into this orphanage. And, what's more, I don't ever expect to have if she's allowed to stay here.

FLORENCE. *(Looking up from her letter; calmly)*

But that's not answering my question, Miss Minnie. Has Anne been impertinent to you?

MINNIE. *(Reluctantly)* No, can't say that she has. But I wouldn't mind that so much. It's that terrific imagination of hers. I've never seen anything like the way that Anne can imagine things. *(Vigorously)* I've gotten so now that every time I see that girl I start to boil inside just like jam. *(She sinks onto chair R. of table.)*

FLORENCE. *(Replacing letter in envelope and sighing wearily)* Poor Anne! *(A sympathetic expression on her face.)*

MINNIE. *(Savagely)* Poor Anne? Poor me, you mean. I'm the one who has to bear the brunt of her flights of fancy. I'm the one who has to go among the children and quiet them after Anne Shirley has almost scared them out of their wits.

FLORENCE. *(Returning to her letters and opening another one)* It's true that Anne has a most vivid imagination. But I'm hoping that with the proper encouragement and because of her gratitude to us she will soon stop all that and think of things in a normal way.

MINNIE. *(Tartly)* Humph! You and I won't live to see that day—if it ever does come.

FLORENCE. *(Protesting)* Oh, come, Miss Minnie.

MINNIE. *(Breaking in firmly)* I tell you I know what I'm talking about. Didn't you hear the disturbance inside a few minutes ago?

FLORENCE. Why, I heard several of the children scream, but after that everything was quiet.

MINNIE. *(Proudly)* Thanks to me! If I hadn't gone inside when I did and quieted their fears some of the little children would be trying to get outside by now.

FLORENCE. Well, for goodness sake, what happened?

MINNIE. It was Anne again, of course. You remember that silver bracelet with the little jade stone set in it that Katie Barth wears?

FLORENCE. Of course. She's had it ever since she first came here. It's an inexpensive little trifle.

MINNIE. The excitement that Anne caused among the children over that bracelet wasn't trifling, you may be sure.

FLORENCE. Why, what did Anne do to Katie?

MINNIE. It seems that Katie mislaid her bracelet and asked Anne if she had seen it. Anne became quite thoughtful for a moment and then her imagination started to work. She gathered all the children around her and half frightened them to death.

FLORENCE. *(In troubled tones)* But how?

MINNIE. She told them that the bracelet came from China and that she was certain the Emperor of China wanted it back because it was once the property of a famous ruler. She even manufactured the name of a Chinese Empress whom, she claimed, owned Katie's bracelet originally.

FLORENCE. *(Frowning)* But there's nothing about that to frighten anybody.

MINNIE. *(Enjoying herself hugely)* Oh, isn't there just? Wait until you hear the rest of her tale. Anne impressed on them that the Emperor of China insisted on having the bracelet back and that he had sent a Chinese killer right here to the orphanage to kill each and every one of them until he discovered the bracelet and was able to take it back to China.

FLORENCE. *(Rising)* But that is absurd.

MINNIE. *(Rising and facing her; firmly)* Not to the children, it wasn't. Anne has such a convincing manner when her imagination starts to work that she'd impress grown-ups, to say nothing of a group of little ones. You should have seen them. They were livid with terror.

FLORENCE. *(Resuming her seat)* I'll have to speak to Anne about this.

MINNIE. *(Scornfully)* Much good that'll do. I've been speaking to her ever since she came here. I just scolded her severely for frightening the other children so outrageously and what d'you suppose her answer was?

FLORENCE. I don't know, I'm sure, but I hope she was duly penitent.

MINNIE. Penitent, nothing! She just looked directly at me and said that she hoped some day I'd enlarge the scope of *my* imagination. *(Drops down on her chair and shakes her head indignantly)* I tell you, Miss Remsen, if you don't get Anne Shirley out of here I'm going to have a complete nervous break-up.

FLORENCE. *(Removing a letter from an envelope and scanning the letter hastily)* Hello! What's this? Why, it's from that nice Mrs. Spencer.

MINNIE. *(Interested)* The one who adopted little Peter Stevenson a few weeks ago?

FLORENCE. *(Nodding assent and continuing to read her letter)* That's right. *(Astonished)* Why, she's coming here today to get another child.

MINNIE. *(Eagerly)* A little sister for Peter, perhaps?

FLORENCE. *(Shaking her head "no")* No, this is for a friend of hers. She wants a girl to send to a family named Cuthbert. She'll tell me all about it when she arrives here, and that ought to be any moment now.

MINNIE. *(Eagerly)* D'you suppose she'd take Anne Shirley off of our hands? Oh, if she only would I'd begin to believe in miracles again.

FLORENCE. *(Thoughtfully)* Well—I don't know. I suppose we might convince Mrs. Spencer that Anne is just the girl for her, but do you know, Miss

Minnie, I'd rather hate to see Anne leave. I know I'd be lonesome for her.

MINNIE. *(Amazed)* You'd—what?

FLORENCE. She's had such a hard time ever since her infancy, my dear. And she's always worked so hard. Nothing is ever too much for Anne to attempt.

MINNIE. *(Witheringly)* You're right about that. And all of her attempts end the same way—destructively. She heads the list of folks who make mistakes permanently.

FLORENCE. But she's such a whimsical little thing, and she does try. I'm sure that she doesn't upset the other children deliberately. *(Loud frightened SCREAMS are heard off R.)*

ANNE. *(Off R.; commanding)* Stop that! Stop it, I say. Stand still and be quiet. (MINNIE *and* FLORENCE *jump up quickly.)*

FLORENCE. *(Bewildered)* I wonder what's going on out there? Go and see, will you, please, Miss Minnie?

MINNIE. *(Determined)* I can tell you in advance what's happening. Anne has the other children upset again. *(She crosses to door R., then turns and faces* FLORENCE*)* Oh, how I wish I was superintendent of this place for just one hour. That would give me time enough to put Anne Shirley out of here. *(She exits quickly.* FLORENCE *resumes her seat behind table, picks up her letter and starts to read it again, a thoughtful expression on her face.)*

ANNE. *(Off R.; tearfully)* But it wasn't my fault—really it wasn't, Miss Minnie. Haven't you any imagination?

MINNIE. *(Off R.; loud and commanding)* Let go of her at once and come with me. It's time Miss Remsen took a hand in things. (FLORENCE *rises and faces door R.* MINNIE *comes through door R., literally dragging* ANNE *with her.* ANNE SHIRLEY *is in her middle teens, but because of her frail build and*

*slight stature she may be played by an older girl
who possesses all of the attributes of extreme youth.
Then, too, make up and youthful dress cause her to
appear extremely juvenile. Grave and solemn in
manner, there is about her an aura of elfish charm,
a whimsical something that completely envelops her.
Life is terribly serious to* ANNE SHIRLEY, *a fact
that causes her to draw heavily upon her imagination. She must be played with utter simplicity. The
more natural she is the more her audiences will love
her and take her to their hearts. Her hair is parted
in the center and hangs down her back in two long
braids. There are several freckles on her nose and a
disturbing few on other parts of her face. Her
dress is severely simple and plain in design. It is
made of some inexpensive homespun and is very
drab in color. The sleeves are tight and plain. It is
the sort of dress that a very poor child would wear
and proclaims her extreme youth. Her stockings are
cheap and ribbed. Flat-heeled black slippers complete her outfit.)*

ANNE. *(Tearfully, as* MINNIE *drags her to* R. *of
table)* I didn't do anything—honest I didn't, Miss
Florence.

FLORENCE. *(To* MINNIE*)* I'll attend to this, Miss
Minnie. Release Anne, please.

MINNIE. *(Withdrawing her hand from* ANNE'S
arm; irately) Humph! Nice carryings on here, I
must say!

FLORENCE. *(Motioning* L.*)* Stand over there,
Anne, and tell me what this is all about.

ANNE. *(Crossing* L. *to front of bench)* It's not
about anything, Miss Florence—really it's not. I'm
afraid I'm just hopelessly old-fashioned. *(Sighs
wearily.)*

FLORENCE. *(Bewildered)* What?

ANNE. *(Looking directly at* FLORENCE*)* It's just
that I never can get Teenie Williams to wash her-

self properly, and I'm afraid I don't like children much unless they're more or less washed.

MINNIE. *(Exasperated)* Well, I never!

FLORENCE. Sit down, Anne. You, too, Miss Minnie. (ANNE *sits on bench* L. MINNIE *sits* R. *of table.* FLORENCE *resumes seat behind table)* Now tell me the details of this latest uprising.

MINNIE. *(Before* ANNE *has a chance to speak)* Poor Teenie Williams has her skin rubbed off and the other children were afraid the same thing would happen to them.

ANNE. *(Shaking her head wearily)* I try so hard to instil Teenie with the desire to be more antiseptic but I'm afraid I don't make much headway. She just seems to enjoy being *mediocum.*

FLORENCE. *(Restraining a desire to laugh)* You mean mediocre, Anne.

ANNE. *(Gratefully)* Oh, Miss Florence, you always know exactly what I mean. That's why you're so conducive.

MINNIE. *(Aghast)* What's that?

ANNE. *(Gravely)* Miss Florence understands me because she allows her imagination to have so much scope. *(To* FLORENCE; *ardently)* You're the only kindred spirit I've met since I came to the orphanage.

MINNIE. *(Bristling indignantly)* Well, I like that! Kindred spirit, indeed!

ANNE. *(Apologetically)* I didn't mean that as anything unkind, Miss Minnie. I'm certain you could be as nice as Miss Florence—that is, almost as nice, if you'd just use your imagination more freely.

MINNIE. *(Beside herself with anger)* Indeed! My imagination suits me, young lady. I have enough of it.

ANNE. *(Gravely)* Oh, but we mustn't ever be satisfied with ourselves. If we are we never can girdle our ambitions. *(To* FLORENCE*)* One must always keep striving for perfection. I always try to like people and be matey. Of course, when you're still young you can't do that so easily. And then, again, there are times when we're all inclined to be disappointed too quickly. (MINNIE *registers disgust.)*

FLORENCE. Anne, I want to—

ANNE. *(Breaking in garrulously)* Don't you think one suffers more when they are grown up, Miss Florence? Especially if they are old and sensitive like you and me?

MINNIE. *(Stiffly)* Humph!

FLORENCE. Listen to me, Anne. How would you like to leave here?

ANNE. *(Rising; slowly)* Leave here? You mean you're going to take me away with you when you go on your vacation? Oh, Miss Florence, that would be simply thrilling!

FLORENCE. *(Shaking her head "no")* No, that wasn't what I meant. Mrs. Alexander Spencer is coming here today to pick out a little girl. She's going to place the girl in a good home and have her legally adopted.

ANNE. *(Excited)* Oh, isn't that wonderful? Did you say her husband's name is Alexander?

FLORENCE. That's right.

ANNE. *(Clapping her hands together delightedly)* Then he must be a leader among men, because I've read of an Alexander in history. I wonder if they were related? I'm certain that anybody named Alexander would be sure to have great scope for imagination.

FLORENCE. *(Silencing her with a gesture)* The girl Mrs. Spencer takes won't live with the Spencers. She is to be placed with a family by the name of Cuthbert.

ANNE. *(Gravely)* I wonder what their first names

are and if they'd be kindred spirits? Oh, Miss Florence, I do so want people to like me.

MINNIE. *(Scornfully)* I don't see why you don't do something about it, then, instead of getting into all sorts of scrapes and being a burden to everybody.

ANNE. *(Tearfully)* Oh, have I been a burden to you, Miss Florence? If I have been, I'm so sorry. I haven't meant to be. Perhaps I'm just too intensive. *(Crosses to just L. of FLORENCE.)*

MINNIE. *(Tartly)* You're too everything, if you ask me.

FLORENCE. *(To MINNIE; reprovingly)* That will do, Miss Minnie. *(To ANNE)* Of course you haven't been a burden, Anne. But you must try to curb your enthusiasms.

ANNE. *(Forlornly)* I do try, but I'm afraid it's hopeless. You see, I'm so homely, and when I look in the mirror I always become conscious of how trying it must be for folks to have such an ugly person around. Then I start in to imagine I'm beautiful and—

FLORENCE. *(Breaking in hastily)* We haven't much time to decide, Anne. Do you want to go with Mrs. Spencer if she'll take you?

ANNE. *(Eagerly)* Do you think she'd allow me to go to school and let me have a dress with puffed sleeves? All my life I've longed for a dress with puffed sleeves.

MINNIE. Why, the idea! Such foolishness!

FLORENCE. *(In kindly tones)* I'll ask Mrs. Spencer if she thinks the Cuthberts would be kind to you. In the meantime it wouldn't do any harm for you to put on your hat and pack your few things so that you could leave at short notice.

ANNE. *(Radiantly)* Oh, Miss Florence, you're the most remarkable person I've ever met. I feel just as though life were opening up before me at last and

I am about to emerge on a great adventure. Don't you think I ought to change my name before I leave here?

MINNIE. *(Aghast)* Change your name? What for?

ANNE. *(Rapturously)* I'd so like to have a name that's romantical—something like Cordelia. I've often imagined that I was Cordelia Shirley instead of Anne, and a handsome knight in armor was attracted by my name and rode up on a purple horse—

MINNIE. *(Breaking in quickly)* Who ever heard of a purple horse?

ANNE. *(Ruefully)* Well, of course, Miss Minnie, if you just won't use your imagination, I'm afraid I could never help you.

MINNIE. *(Irately)* You help me, eh? That's good, that is. You'd better start trying to help yourself, Miss.

FLORENCE. *(Smiling kindly at* ANNE*)* You get ready, Anne, and I'll call you when I want you to meet Mrs. Spencer. And remember, you're to be on your good behavior the rest of the day.

ANNE. *(Joyously)* Oh, you needn't worry about that, Miss Florence. I'll be as quiet as we always *pretend* to be when Miss Minnie comes through the dormitory to see if we are asleep. *(Laughs lightly; skips out* R.*)*

MINNIE. *(Scornfully)* Purple horse! Cordelia Shirley! What next? *(DOORBELL rings off* R.*)*

FLORENCE. That must be Mrs. Spencer now. Will you let her in, please, Miss Minnie?

MINNIE. *(Rising and crossing to door* R.*)* I surely hope Anne behaves herself and doesn't get into any scrapes while Mrs. Spencer is here. *(Exits* R. FLORENCE *pats at her hair and rises, coming down stage to below table* C. MINNIE *enters* R. *and stands just above door; loudly)* Mrs. Alexander Spencer to see Miss Remsen.

(MRS. ALEXANDER SPENCER, *a short, stout woman in her early fifties, enters* R., *breathing heavily. She is obviously a small town housewife with a kind heart and a desire to help others. She is dressed in a coat suit that has long since been outmoded, a hat with a few colored flowers on it; carries a purse and an umbrella.*)

FLORENCE. *(As* MRS. SPENCER *enters)* It's so nice seeing you again, Mrs. Spencer. Sit down, won't you? *(Indicates chair behind table)* I hope you're well and enjoying your adopted son.

MRS. SPENCER. *(Crossing up to behind table and sitting)* I'm as well as can be expected but I suffer somethin' terrible from shortness o' breath. (FLORENCE *sits* L. *of table.* MINNIE *takes over and sits* R. *of table.* MRS. SPENCER *faces* MINNIE) Did you ever suffer from that?

FLORENCE. *(Pointedly)* Hardly. Miss Minnie has had a few ailments, but shortness of breath has never been among them. (MINNIE *darts an angry glance at* FLORENCE.)

MRS. SPENCER. *(Complaining)* Mr. Spencer says he never can notice that I'm short of breath, but you know how men are. Just 'cause I don't go 'round complainin' all the time he thinks I'm as healthy as can be.

FLORENCE. *(In businesslike tones)* Now, about this girl your friend wants to adopt. Did she tell you just how old she wants the girl to be?

MRS. SPENCER. She didn't tell me anythin'. I ain't seen Marilla Cuthbert in ages. You see, she lives miles away from me. But Nancy, you know, Nancy Spencer—she's my husband's niece and a most flighty girl if there ever was one, though I shouldn't say it considerin' that she's a relation— *(Pauses and breathes heavily)* Oh, dear, I'm all out o' breath. I just can't hardly talk at all.

FLORENCE. *(Anxiously)* Are these Cuthberts in a position to take care of a girl and educate her?

MRS. SPENCER. *(Nodding vigorously)* Oh, yes, indeedy. Matthew Cuthbert has a tremendous farm and is quite well fixed.

MINNIE. *(Eagerly)* And does his wife want to take a little girl to raise?

MRS. SPENCER. *(Chuckling heartily)* His wife? Matthew Cuthbert ain't got any wife. He has a sister, name o' Marilla. She runs Matthew's life for him and never would allow him to even see a girl, much less court one. Whatever Marilla says goes. She runs the roost. I'd tell you more about her if I wasn't so short o' breath and didn't find it so hard to talk.

FLORENCE. What sort of disposition has Miss Cuthbert, Mrs. Spencer?

MRS. SPENCER. *(Enjoying herself hugely)* The wrong sort. If there ever was a person whose milk o' human kindness got soured in her veins when she was young, her name is Marilla Cuthbert. If she ever forgot to be glum and stern she'd be so angry she's never forgive herself. Now, Matthew, her brother, is just the opposite—but it don't do no good, 'cause he's never expressed an opinion o' his own in all his life—he wouldn't dare. *(Taking a deep breath)* Oh, dear, I wish it wasn't so hard for me to say a few words. I'd like to tell you more.

MINNIE. *(Leaning forward; eagerly)* Of course it's just possible that this Miss Cuthbert has changed since you last saw her, Mrs. Spencer, isn't it?

MRS. SPENCER. *(Witheringly)* Change? Marilla Cuthbert change? *I'd like to see the person who could make her over!* I'm not sayin' that she's not a respectable, hard-workin' woman who never misses a church service and contributes regular to The Ladies' Aid. She ain't never had any gayety in her life and she ain't never goin' to let anybody 'round her have any, neither.

MINNIE. *(Hastily)* A very proper spirit, I'm sure. She sounds like the very sort of person who'll be successful with a girl like Anne.

MRS. SPENCER. *(Suspiciously)* Anne? What kinda girl is she? Nothin' wrong with her, is there? I ain't aimin' to do anythin' that's goin' to bring Marilla's wrath down on my head. If Nancy wasn't such a rattle-brained girl I'd have made her tell me just what sort of a girl Marilla wants. *(Taking a deep breath)* Oh, dear, I wish it wasn't so hard for me to talk. *(To* FLORENCE*)* I don't want to send Marilla any girl that ain't well-behaved and lady-like. You understand.

FLORENCE. *(Reassuringly)* You've nothing to worry about on that score, I assure you, Mrs. Spencer. Anne is a perfect little lady. True, she does talk a lot—

MRS. SPENCER. *(Breaking in quickly)* She does? I'd say that's in her favor. I wish I could talk as much as I'd like to. *(Sighs heavily.)*

FLORENCE. *(Proudly)* Anne has only been with us for four months, but she's a very hard worker. She never shirks a responsibility. She is always anxious to bathe the other children and wash them—

MINNIE. *(Breaking in firmly)* Yes, indeed. I can vouch for that. She's so thorough when she bathes the children that she rubs their skin off.

MRS. SPENCER. Well, she'll have plenty o' chores to do at the Cuthberts. They have a mighty big place called Green Gables, and Marilla keeps it as clean as snow. She told that Nancy to give me a message, but o' course Miss Nancy forgot all about what it was. It's a wonder she remembered to tell me that Marilla wants to adopt a girl. *(Taking a deep breath)* Oh, dear, I just have the most awful pain every time I try to say a few words.

FLORENCE. *(Rising)* Perhaps you'd better bring Anne in now, Miss Minnie. I'm sure Mrs. Spencer will fall in love with her at first sight.

MINNIE. *(Rising; with pretended warmth)* I'm sure she will. And the more she sees of the little dear the more she'll love her. She's so restful and quiet. *(Loud GLASS CRASH is heard off R., followed by the SCREAMS of several voices.)*

MRS. SPENCER. *(Rising; alarmed)* Mercy days, what was that?

ANNE. *(Off R.; tearfully)* Oh, Miss Florence, I didn't mean to do it, honest I didn't. It just happened. (MINNIE *and* FLORENCE *exchange anxious glances.)*

MRS. SPENCER. Who's that? (ANNE *rushes on breathlessly,* R. *She has donned a faded sailor hat that is most becoming.)*

FLORENCE. *(As she sees* ANNE; *anxiously)* What is it, Anne? What's happened?

ANNE. *(Coming over to* L. *of* FLORENCE; *tearfully)* Oh, Miss Florence, I'm afraid I'll have to stay here now and work for you forever to make up for breaking your favorite vase.

MINNIE. *(Irately)* You broke that glass vase on the mantel?

ANNE. *(Tearfully)* Yes. You see, I was so elated about going to a home of my own and being able to go to school and everything that my imagination just started running riot. I fancied that I was a great queen and that I was giving a farewell party to all my loyal subjects. Of course I had to have a scepter, so I just picked up that tall vase and started to wave it around, when suddenly it fell out of my hand and crashed to the floor in a million pieces— Oh, it was just too tragical for words.

FLORENCE. *(Placing an arm around* ANNE *comfortingly)* Well, you mustn't feel too badly about it,

Anne. After all, it's not as though you broke it purposely.

ANNE. *(Smiling through her tears)* Oh, Miss Florence, you're just an angel. I'll never forget you —never. (MINNIE *darts an anxious look at* FLORENCE *and clears her throat significantly.)*

FLORENCE. *(Hastily)* This is Mrs. Spencer, Anne. She's going to take you away with her if she likes you. (MINNIE *crosses and looks off* R. MRS. SPENCER *comes down* R. *to below table.)*

ANNE. *(Crossing to* L. *of* MRS. SPENCER *and smiling up at her)* Oh, I know I'm going to like you because you're a kindred spirit. Do you suppose the lady you're going to take me to will let me have a dress with puffed sleeves?

MRS. SPENCER. *(Bewildered)* Puffed sleeves? Well, I can't say as to that. She'll have plenty for you to do, that I can tell you.

ANNE. *(Enthusiastically)* Oh, I won't mind that. Where does she live, this lady?

MRS. SPENCER. At Avonlea in a big house that has always been called Green Gables.

ANNE. *(Clapping her hands together delightedly)* Green Gables! Oh, what a gorgeous name. I can just picture it. The house once belonged to a King and Queen. She was real beautiful with pure gold hair that rippled back from her alabaster brow and— *(Pausing; gravely)* What is an alabaster brow, anyhow? I never have been able to find out.

MINNIE. *(Greatly upset)* Tch! Tch! I'd better go and see if the others are all right. I don't want them to cut their hands on that broken glass. *(Exits* R.)

MRS. SPENCER. *(Smiling)* Well, I can see that you are a great talker, Anne. You do use a lot o' big words, too, don't you? Strange as it may seem, I like to hear you talk.

ANNE. *(Smiling happily)* Oh, I'm so glad. I know you and I are going to get along together just fine,

It's such a relief to talk when one wants to and not be told that young folks should be seen and not heard. I've had that said to me a million times. And folks laugh at me because I use big words. But if one has big ideas they have to use big words to express them, don't they?

MRS. SPENCER. *(Dubiously)* I can't say that I'm sure how Miss Cuthbert will take to you, Anne. It might be that you'll be able to talk her down, but I doubt it. She hasn't got much to say, but when she does speak everybody jumps.

ANNE. Oh, I'm sure I'll like her. From your description she sounds as though she has a definite personality. That always appeals strongly to me. I don't like people who are wishy-washy, do you?

MRS. SPENCER. *(Doubtfully)* Marilla is definite, all right, but I can't be sure how you'll get on together. However, there'd be the same risk no matter who I sent to her, and since she's asked for a girl it might as well be you, I suppose. *(Taking a deep breath)* If I wasn't so short o' breath I'd ask you a lot more questions.

FLORENCE. *(Tactfully)* I'm sure Anne will tell you anything you want to know during your journey.

MRS. SPENCER. I'll send a telegram to Matthew to meet your train at the other end.

ANNE. *(Greatly awed)* You—you mean that I'm going to ride on a train all by myself? (MRS. SPENCER *nods.)* Oh, how perfectly beautiful! I'll imagine that it's my own fiery chariot and that I'm going forth to find out about all the things that I've asked questions about and that nobody could ever answer. There must be a thousand of them. And I'll just imagine that I have on a dress with the widest puffed sleeves that any girl ever had and that everybody is admiring me for my beauty. Of course, I know that I'm ugly and that nobody will ever marry me except, maybe, a foreign missionary.

FLORENCE. *(Exchanging an amused glance with* MRS. SPENCER*)* Why, Anne, what makes you think a foreign missionary would marry you?

ANNE. *(Gravely)* Well, I don't suppose they can afford to be too fussy. Don't you agree with me, Mrs. Spencer? Oh, when I think of getting on a train it makes me feel glad to be alive. It's such an interesting world, isn't it? There'll be so much scope for imagination on this trip. But am I talking too much? I can stop when I make up my mind to, although I'll admit it is a bit difficult.

(WARN Curtain.)

MRS. SPENCER. *(Astonished)* I never heard the beat of it. I believe she could even talk my Alexander down. And he thinks that I talk too much. *(Crossing to door* R.*)* Well, come along, child. You'd better get talked out now because I don't know that you'll have time to talk when Marilla Cuthbert once puts you to work. *(Chuckles and exits* R.*)*

ANNE. *(Throwing her arms around* FLORENCE *and hugging her)* Goodbye, dear Miss Florence. Parting is such sweet sorrow. I'd better go quickly, for I'm afraid I'm going to cry. I'll write to you whenever I can and—and— Oh, dear, it's all so conducive. *(Stifles a sob, rushes* R. *and exits quickly.)*

FLORENCE. *(Crossing and calling off* R.*)* Goodbye, Anne. Do try to be a good girl and mind what folks tell you. Goodbye, Mrs. Spencer. *(She waves off* R. *several times, then crosses to below table.)*

MINNIE. *(As she enters* R.; *joyfully)* She's saying her goodbyes now to the children. In a few minutes we'll be rid of her forever.

FLORENCE. *(As though thinking aloud)* Poor Anne! Poor little orphan! I can't help but pity her.

MINNIE. *(R. of* FLORENCE; *tartly)* I pity the poor Cuthberts who are going to take her in. She'll make their lives miserable with her eternal chatter.

FLORENCE. *(Smiling)* Well, there's one thing that even you'll have to admit, Miss Minnie.

MINNIE. *(Skeptically)* What's that?

FLORENCE. *(Firmly)* Wherever Anne Shirley is there'll never be a dull moment. *(She laughs lightly as the Curtain falls swiftly to denote a lapse of time.* AUTHOR'S NOTE: *The instant the Curtain falls, MINNIE and FLORENCE exit hastily. The small inset and the furniture used in the above scene are removed as quickly as possible so that the Curtain need only remain lowered for a very short interval. There must not be a long wait.)*

END OF SCENE I

SCENE II

SCENE: *The sitting room of the Cuthberts' home, Green Gables, Avonlea.*

TIME: *Late afternoon of the following day.*

DESCRIPTION OF SET: *A spacious room that is replete with a quaint atmosphere. All of the furniture and furnishings have been handed down from previous generations. It is the type of room that we were ushered into when we first visited our grandparents as children. A soft carpet covers the floor, with a few rag rugs over it to hide the worn places. In the rear wall, direct Center, is an arch that leads out to a hallway; an interior backing. Through the arch and off Right leads to the exterior; through the arch and off Left leads to the bedrooms and up-stairs portion of the house. In the Left wall are* two doors, both with interior backings. The door well upstage, L.2, leads to a seldom-used parlor, while the door down stage, L.1, leads to the dining room and kitchen. A screen door in the Center of the Right wall leads out to a balustrade; garden or exterior backing. A doorbell ring off stage up Right. (NOTE: This should be an old-fashioned bell—the sort that jangles.) Near rear wall and Right of arch is a stand table covered with a doily. A family album rests on the table. In extreme upper Left corner is a whatnot with several miscellaneous articles in it. A rocking chair near rear wall and Left of arch. In extreme lower Right wall a built-in settee with a few cushions on it. An armchair in extreme lower Left corner. Well down stage and Right of Center is a round table with three old-fashioned chairs surrounding it. On an angle with this table, but Left of Center, a real old sofa with a few cushions to decorate it. An overstuffed hassock just below sofa. Most of the chairs in the room have antimacassars on their backs. Old-fashioned oil paintings in wooden boxes on the walls, family portraits, bric-a-brac ornaments to dress the stage at the discretion of the director. All LIGHTS on stage full up. LIGHTS outside of screen door to denote waning daylight. The room is scrupulously clean and has a homey charm to be found only among people who are attached to their dwellings.

DISCOVERED AT RISE: MARILLA CUTHBERT, a tall, well-built woman in her late forties, stands at screen door R., looking off stage. She is a woman of rigid conscience who has her own ideas as to the fitness of things. Her hair is streaked with grey and is gathered in a small *knot at the back with a few wire hairpins to hold the knot in place.* MARILLA *is always neat and tidy, but there is never an attempt at ostentation. Her gingham housedress is made along conventional lines. Her black shoes are of the buttoned type. She has her knitting and knitting needles in her hand. Beneath her stern exterior there is a human quality lurking and trying to make itself evident, but* MARILLA *spends her life trying to hide this from the world. Her real nature is masked by a gruffness, a strictness that is difficult to penetrate. The instant the Curtain rises,* MARILLA *pushes the screen door open.*

MARILLA. *(Calling off* R. *loudly)* Mrs. Barry— Oh, Mrs. Barry! Won't you come in and set for awhile?

MRS. BARRY. *(Off* R.*)* Well, I'll come in, but I can't stay long. I'm on my way to the station.

(MARILLA *crosses over to just below sofa* L. *of* C. MRS. MILDRED BARRY, *a fine-appearing woman in her late forties, enters through screen door* R. *She is cultured and refined in manner, possessed of a lovely smile and a frank and sincere nature. Her summer frock is decidedly becoming and her hat and all of her accessories are in excellent taste.)*

MARILLA. *(As* MRS. BARRY *enters)* Do set for awhile. Matthew's not here today.

MRS. BARRY. *(As she crosses to* L. *of table* R.C. *and sits; knowingly)* You're the second person to acquaint me with that fact. I met Mrs. Lynde as I was driving along, Miss Marilla.

MARILLA. *(Aghast)* How on earth did Rachel Lynde know that Matthew wasn't here? *(Angrily)*

That's a foolish question to ask. That woman knows what a body is doing before they even think of doing it.

MRS. BARRY. She does seem to know a great deal.

MARILLA. *(Sitting on sofa; irately)* She's the worst busybody I ever saw. You'd think that with eight children to care for she'd have enough to do to keep her mind out of other folks' affairs.

MRS. BARRY. *(Soothingly)* I wouldn't let Mrs. Rachel worry me if I were you.

MARILLA. *(Loudly and excitedly)* She don't worry me. I never give her a thought. But I do hate to have folks prying into my business. *(Anxiously)* Did she tell you why Matthew isn't at home today?

MRS. BARRY. *(Shaking her head "no")* No, she didn't. I only stopped to talk to her for a minute or so.

MARILLA. *(Relievedly)* Thank fortune she hasn't found out yet what Matthew's errand is. But she will, of course. Just give her time and she'll find out anything.

MRS. BARRY. I just won't allow her to upset me.

MARILLA. *(Angrily)* I've never had any time for her since the first time I met her years ago. She took one look at me and told me I was ugly. I've never forgotten it.

MRS. BARRY. *(Sympathetically)* What a dreadful thing for one person to say to another.

MARILLA. *(Clearing her throat as though ashamed of her outburst)* Humph! Not that I lay claim to beauty or ever think about it. There are other things in this world outside of that.

MRS. BARRY. Indeed there are. I always try to avoid Mrs. Lynde as much as possible.

MARILLA. *(Tartly)* 'Tain't possible, far as I'm concerned. She's always sticking her nose in here when she ain't wanted.

(MRS. RACHEL LYNDE, *a tall, thin, angular woman of uncertain years, sticks her head in through screen door* R. *She is the village busybody and is never so happy as when prying into other people's affairs. Wears an outmoded coat suit of a forgotten era, a small hat is perched on the back of her head for comedy effect and she carries a large purse and a parasol.*)

RACHEL. *(In high, shrill tones)* May I come in? I won't be disturbin' you, will I?

MARILLA. *(Grudgingly)* No, of course not. Come in, Rachel.

MRS. BARRY. *(Rising)* I was just going.

RACHEL. *(Coming down to* R. *of table* R.C.*)* On your way to the station to meet your Diana, ain't you, Missus Barry?

MRS. BARRY. *(Nodding assent)* Yes, my daughter is arriving home today. She's had a lovely trip, according to her letters. I'll be so happy to have her with me again. (MARILLA *attacks her knitting vigorously.*)

RACHEL. *(Dropping into chair* R. *of table* L.C.*)* That's what you'd oughta have here in your house, Marilla. A little girl. It would be comp'ny for you.

MARILLA. *(As though the very idea were poisonous)* A girl in my house? A girl to break things and scatter crumbs over everything and that I'd have to spend my life cleaning up after? No, sir-ee! I've never seen the girl yet that I'd tolerate.

RACHEL. *(Placing her parasol and purse on table* R.C.*)* Reckon you'd get used to havin' a girl here after awhile if you had to.

MARILLA. *(Jumping up; vigorously)* Reckon I just wouldn't. And there's no sense in talking about it, 'cause it will never be. *(To* MRS. BARRY*)* 'Scuse me. I've got to do something in the kitchen. I'll be right back. *(Crosses and exits hastily* L.I.*)*

RACHEL. *(Complainingly)* Humph! Marilla sure is sot in her ways, ain't she? It's caused her a heap o' unhappiness. Now, if she had come to me for advice—

MRS. BARRY. *(Breaking in quickly)* You'll have to excuse me, Mrs. Lynde. *(Rises)* I don't want to miss Diana's train. *(Starts up stage.)*

RACHEL. *(Rising; eagerly)* Just a minute, Missus Barry. *(Her voice halts MRS. BARRY, who turns and faces her)* Did Marilla tell you where Matthew went today?

MRS. BARRY. No, she didn't. And of course I wouldn't ask her.

RACHEL. *(Anxiously)* Didn't she even drop a hint?

MRS. BARRY. *(Shaking her head "no")* Not even a hint. And truthfully, I'm not at all curious.

RACHEL. *(Disappointed)* I ain't curious, neither, but I'd just like to know. Must be somethin' terrible unusual for Matthew Cuthbert to get himself all cleaned up an' put on his best store clothes on a weekday. I ain't never known him to do it before.

MRS. BARRY. *(Crossing up to door R.; pointedly)* I'm sure Miss Marilla won't mind telling you where he went and why, when you *ask her about it.*

RACHEL. *(Crossing up to behind table R.C. and facing MRS. BARRY)* We-el, I don't know as to that. Marilla can be mighty persnicketty when she wants to be, which she usually does. That woman is so mean by nature that when she puts up sweet pickles they turn sour without her doin' a thing about it.

MRS. BARRY. *(Stiffly)* I've always found her to be most affable.

RACHEL. *(Nodding vigorously)* Ain't that what I just said? She's so strict an' stern like that folks just shun her. I'm the only friend she has, an' that's 'cause I'm so easy-goin'.

MRS. BARRY. *(Icily)* Tell Miss Marilla that I

couldn't wait, please. Good afternoon. *(She exits quickly R.)*

RACHEL. *(Tossing her head indignantly)* Humph. *(Inspects the top of table R.C. for dust, then crosses up to extreme L. and examines the contents of the whatnot in a prying manner, then goes over to R. of arch and inspects the stand table, picking up the album and opening same. MARILLA enters L.I, carrying a geranium plant and also her knitting.)*

MARILLA. *(Pausing in front of door L.I; harshly)* Well, Rachel?

RACHEL. *(Closing album quickly and replacing it on stand table and coming down to L. of table R.C.)* I—er—I was just lookin' at that old album, Marilla. *(Sits on chair L. of table R.C.)* I do hope nothin' happens to Matthew on his long drive. You didn't ask *my* advice, o' course, but if you had I'd o' told you not to let him go alone. *(Settles back in her chair.)*

MARILLA. *(Crossing R. to below table R.C. and placing plant on table)* Nothing's going to happen to my brother. I'm expecting him home any minute now. *(Looking around anxiously)* Where's Mrs. Barry?

RACHEL. *(Irately)* Gone to the station to meet Diana. If she'd asked *my* advice, an' o' course she didn't, I'd have told her that little girls like Diana oughta have somebody travel with them.

MARILLA. *(Crossing back to sofa and sitting)* I'm sorry she didn't wait. I wanted to give her that plant for Diana. *(Starts to knit industriously.)*

RACHEL. *(Clearing her throat)* Er—Matthew musta gone quite a distance to stay away this long.

MARILLA. *(Without looking up from her knitting)* Yes, quite a distance. How is Mr. Lynde, Rachel?

RACHEL. *(Hastily)* Oh, same as usual. *(Eagerly)* I've never known Matthew to leave his work this way before. Must be somethin' mighty important to take him away.

MARILLA. *(Lightly)* Yes, it must be.

RACHEL. *(Agog with curiosity)* I saw him drive away early this mornin'.

MARILLA. *(Stiffly)* I know when he left, Rachel.

RACHEL. 'Course you do. He wouldn't o' left without your say so.

MARILLA. That's where you're wrong. Matthew was more eager to leave than I was to have him go.

RACHEL. *(Astonished)* Lan's sake, I ain't never known Matthew to be eager 'bout anythin'. You won't mind tellin' me where he's gone and why, will you, Marilla?

MARILLA. *(Putting down her knitting; resignedly)* I suppose I might as well tell you. You'll find out anyhow. *(Casually)* Matthew's gone over to meet the train at Bright River. We're getting a child from the orphanage at Hopeton.

RACHEL. *(Jumping up as though she had been shot)* A child? You mean, a little *girl?*

MARILLA. *(Firmly)* I don't mean anything of the kind. How many times must I tell you that I wouldn't have a girl in my house? Matthew is bringing a boy back with him.

RACHEL. *(Astonished)* A boy—from an orphanage? Are—are you in earnest, Marilla?

MARILLA. *(Calmly)* Yes, of course I am.

RACHEL. *(Folding her hands in front of her; thoroughly nonplussed)* Gettin' a boy from an orphan asylum! Well, I must say! The world seems to be turnin' upside down. Nothin'll ever surprise me after this. Well!

MARILLA. *(Quietly)* I've—that is, *we've* been thinking of it for some time; all winter, in fact. But we didn't decide definitely until a few weeks ago.

RACHEL. *(Crossing to R. of sofa)* But what on earth ever put such an idee into your head?

MARILLA. Nancy Spencer was here a short time ago and she told us that Mrs. Alexander Spencer had adopted such a lovely boy from the Hopeton Orphan Asylum. So Matthew and I have been talking it over. His heart bothers him at times. He's getting on in years.

RACHEL. *(Agog with curiosity)* But what's Matthew's heart got to do with adoptin' a boy?

MARILLA. Why, you know how hard it is to get good farm help—in fact, it's almost impossible. Boys all want to go to the city to work these days. So we decided to take a boy to raise and let him help with the farm work.

RACHEL. *(Firmly)* Well, Marilla, I'll just tell you plain that I think you're doin' a mighty risky thing —mighty risky.

MARILLA. *(Protesting)* But—

RACHEL. *(Continuing as though she hadn't been interrupted)* You've no idee o' what you're gettin'. You're bringin' a strange child into the house an' you don't know a single thing 'bout him nor what his disposition's like nor how he's likely to turn out.

MARILLA. Yes, that's true, but—

RACHEL. *(Continuing hastily)* Why, only last week I was readin' 'bout a boy who was adopted by a family from an orphanage an' he *set fire to the house at night*—did it 'a' purpose, too.

MARILLA. *(Scoffing)* That's silly. Nobody's going to set fire to our house.

RACHEL. *(Warningly)* A body never knows, what with the things you hear o' nowadays. I know o' another case where an adopted boy used to suck the eggs. They just couldn't break him o' it. If you had asked *my* advice in the matter, which you didn't do, I'd o' said for mercy's sake not to think o' such a thing—I most certainly would.

MARILLA. *(Resuming her knitting)* I'll admit there's something in what you say, Rachel. But you see, it's so seldom Matthew sets his mind on anything that when he does I always feel it's my duty to give in. And he just longed to adopt an orphan. He has for years.

RACHEL. *(Dubiously)* Well, I hope it'll turn out all right, but ten chances to one it won't. Only don't say I didn't warn you if he causes you misery or puts strychnine in the well. I read o' a case where an orphan asylum child did that, and before they knew it the whole family died in fearful agonies. Only it was a girl in this instance.

MARILLA. *(Complacently)* Well, we're not getting a girl, thank goodness. I'd never even consider taking a girl to bring up.

RACHEL. *(Taking a step closer to sofa)* Seems to me you'd have wanted to go to the orphanage and pick out your own boy.

MARILLA. *(Lightly)* Oh, I'd trust to Mrs. Spencer's judgment. She's right smart.

RACHEL. *(Witheringly)* Well, I wouldn't trust that Nancy in my sight, much less outa it. She's so flighty an' rattle-brained! I've never met the like o' her. *(Shaking her head)* I just can't get over the whole affair. Of all things that ever were or ever will be! *(Rushes up to R. door, leaving her purse and parasol on table R.C. and forgetting them in her haste. She turns and faces MARILLA; firmly)* It seems uncanny, somehow, to think o' a child at Green Gables. But don't say I didn't warn you, Marilla. If you'd asked *my* advice—but there, you didn't. If it does turn out that you're murdered in your beds, don't say that Rachel Lynde didn't tell you. *(Tosses her head knowingly and exits R. MARILLA heaves a worried sigh and attacks her knitting vigorously, a worried expression on her face. MATTHEW CUTHBERT enters C. from R. and stands in arch inspecting the room cautiously. He is a short man in his late fifties. The top of his head is entirely bald and the remaining fringe of hair on the sides is pure white. Generous, charitable, benevolent, his kindly nature is reflected in his face. The world would be an easier place to live in if there were more Matthews. Diffident and shy, he has seldom dared to venture an opinion and has been completely under* MARILLA'S *dominance. He wears his best suit, a conventional blue serge business suit, white shirt, stiff white collar, black string bow tie, black shoes. A heavy, old-fashioned gold watch chain is worn across his vest. As he enters he removes an old-fashioned straw hat that has a wide rolling brim.)*

MATTHEW. *(Standing in arch* C. *and mopping his forehead nervously with a large handkerchief. He clears his throat)* We-ll, Marilla. I'm here.

MARILLA. *(Dropping her knitting on sofa and jumping up quickly)* Matthew! *(Crosses up a few steps and regards him anxiously)* Well, where's the boy? (MATTHEW *clears his throat again nervously.* MARILLA *takes up stage a few more steps, standing* L.C.; *sternly)* Can't you talk? Say something! Didn't you meet the boy? Wasn't he at the train?

MATTHEW. *(Fearfully)* Well, I can't say that he was and I can't say that he wasn't.

MARILLA. *(Impatiently)* You mean that they didn't send him after all?

MATTHEW. Well, I ain't saying that they did and I ain't saying that they didn't.

MARILLA. *(Crossing up to* L. *of arch; angrily)* Matthew Cuthbert, you're the most provoking man I ever met. Tell me what's happened.

MATTHEW. *(In a frenzy of nervousness)* Well, I don't know as I'd better but I'm afraid I'll hafta. Prepare yourself for a shock, Marilla.

MARILLA. *(Witheringly)* I'm used to shocks. Come, Matthew, get it over with. Tell me the worst. It must be dreadful.

MATTHEW. Well, I ain't saying that it is and I

ain't saying that it ain't. You can see for yourself. *(He turns and motions off* R. *as though beckoning somebody to enter.* MARILLA *takes over* L. *a few steps.* MATTHEW *takes over to* R. *of arch as* ANNE *enters slowly* C. *from* R. *and stands in arch. She is dressed exactly as she was in previous scene and continues to wear the faded sailor hat. She carries a small, outmoded valise in one hand and regards* MARILLA *eagerly.)*

MARILLA. *(Looking at* ANNE *as though she can hardly believe her eyes)* Matthew Cuthbert, who's that? Where is the boy?

MATTHEW. *(Fearfully)* There wasn't any boy, Marilla. There was only *her.*

MARILLA. *(Loudly and excitedly)* But there must have been a boy. I distinctly told Nancy Spencer that I must have a boy.

ANNE. *(Swallowing nervously)* Please, ma'am, Mrs. Alexander Spencer said that Miss Nancy stated definitely that you told her you wanted a girl. That's why she picked me.

MARILLA. *(Wrathfully)* I might have known that Nancy Spencer couldn't get anything straight. Well, this is a pretty piece of business, I must say. *(She crosses down to below sofa.)*

ANNE. *(Coming down to* R. *of sofa and smiling at* MARILLA*)* I just know I'm going to love it here at Green Gables and I'm sure there'll be plenty of scope for imagination. It's the most beautiful house I've ever seen. I'm certain that it will be terribly conducive.

MARILLA. *(Looking at her, bewildered)* What?

MATTHEW. *(Coming down to* R. *of* ANNE*)* She talks a deal but she don't mean any harm, Marilla.

MARILLA. *(Bluntly)* But she's not a boy and she can't stay here. That's settled. (MATTHEW *takes over* R. *a few steps.)*

ANNE. *(Facing* MARILLA; *tearfully)* You don't

want me! Just because I'm not a boy. I might have expected it. Nobody ever did want me since the first day I was born. I might have known it was all too beautiful to last. I might have known I'd never be able to be happy as other girls are. Oh, I'm going to cry. *(She drops her valise on floor* R. *of her and sobs loudly.)*

MARILLA. *(Darting a hopeless glance at* MATTHEW) Well, well, there's no need to cry so about it, is there, Matthew?

MATTHEW. *(Eyeing* ANNE *thoughtfully)* Well, I can't say that there is and I can't say that there ain't.

ANNE. *(Stifling her sobs and facing* MARILLA *tremblingly)* Yes, there is need. *You* would cry, too, if you were an orphan and had come to a place you thought was going to be home and found that they didn't want you because you— *(Pauses, then wailing loudly)* Oh, this is the most *tragical* moment of my life! (MATTHEW *crosses down to in front of built-in settee* R. ANNE *stumbles over to chair* L. *of table* R.C, *sinks onto same and sobs loudly.)*

MARILLA. *(Taking over to* L. *of* ANNE; *harsh and commanding)* Stop that crying this instant. (ANNE *makes a great effort and stops sobbing abruptly.)* We won't turn you out of doors right now. You can stay at least until tomorrow. What's your name?

ANNE. *(Looking directly at* MARILLA; *eagerly)* Will you please call me Cordelia? (MATTHEW *drops onto settee and places his hat on same.)*

MARILLA. *(Shrilly)* Cordelia? Is that your name?

ANNE. *(Reluctantly)* No-o-o, it's not exactly my name but I would love so to be called Cordelia. It's such a perfectly elegant name.

MARILLA. *(Sternly)* If Cordelia isn't your name, what is it?

ANNE. *(Slowly)* Anne Shirley. *(Jumping up and facing* MARILLA *pleadingly)* But oh, please call me

Cordelia. It can't matter to you what you call me if I'm only going to be here a little while, can it? And Anne is such an unromantic name.

MARILLA. *(Grimly)* Unromantic, fiddlesticks. (MATTHEW *chuckles softly.* MARILLA *glares at him and he stops chuckling abruptly)* Anne is a real good plain sensible name. You've no need to be ashamed of it.

ANNE. *(Firmly)* Oh, I'm not ashamed of it—truly I'm not. But I get so tired of plain sensible things, don't you? When I was real young I imagined I was Geraldine; then, as I got to be real old, I came to like Cordelia better. But if you must call me Anne, please call me Anne spelled with an "e." *(Her glance pleads with* MARILLA.*)*

MARILLA. *(Irately)* What difference does it make how it's spelled?

ANNE. *(With great earnestness)* Oh, it makes a tremendous difference, really it does. It *looks* so much more distinguished. If you'll only call me Anne spelled with an "e" I'll try to reconcile myself to not being called Cordelia.

MARILLA. *(Crossing to sofa and sitting; witheringly)* Very well, Anne spelled with an "e." Tell me something about yourself.

ANNE. *(Resuming her seat* L. *of table* R.C.*)* Would you like to hear about my journey here on the fiery charger and how a Royal Prince accosted me and told me he thought I was the most interesting person he'd ever encountered because he said I was so intensive?

MARILLA. *(Bewildered)* Fiery charger? Royal Prince? *(To* MATTHEW*)* What on earth does she mean, Matthew? Do you understand her?

MATTHEW. *(Scratching the side of his head; bewildered)* Well, I can't say that I do and I can't say that I don't.

ANNE. *(Rapturously)* Oh, Matthew and I understand each other perfectly. The instant I saw him at the station I knew that he was a kindred spirit. I feel that I've known him forever and ever. Do you ever feel that way about people? Why, I know Matthew so well by now that I can read his mind.

MARILLA. *(Tartly)* Hm, that wouldn't be very difficult. *(MATTHEW clears his throat nervously.)* Matthew, take her valise outside in the hall, and you might as well take her hat, too. You won't be able to drive her back until tomorrow, that's certain. *(MATTHEW rises, crosses up to L. of ANNE, who removes her hat and hands it to him, thanking him with a smile. He picks up ANNE'S valise and crosses up to arch, where he exits C. to R., taking the hat and the valise with him.)*

ANNE. *(To MARILLA; delightedly)* Well, I didn't have the trip for nothing. At least I met Matthew and I know I'll never meet another human being half so kind. And I saw The White Way of Delight and The Lake of the Shining Water and—

MARILLA. *(Breaking in in puzzled tones)* Sakes alive, what *are* you talking about?

ANNE. *(Gravely)* You see, I've had to learn early in life that things aren't so bad if you just *imagine* that they're not. So when I saw the beautiful lake that Matthew drove me past, I just imagined that it was The Lake of the Shining Water. It's so much fun giving beautiful names to things. It makes them twice as beautiful as they are.

MARILLA. *(Gruffly)* I never heard of such a thing.

ANNE. *(Astonished)* Haven't you ever imagined things? I should think you would, you've such a beautiful house here. Oh, if I could just stay here it would be ever so easy to imagine all sorts of lovely things.

MARILLA. *(Amazed)* Then all that talk about fiery chargers and royal princes was just fancy? You made it all up yourself?

ANNE. *(Nodding vigorously)* Of course. You see, nobody paid any attention to me on the train so I just had the grandest time *imagining* that I was a Princess and—

MARILLA. *(Breaking in sternly)* I wish you'd stop that and just imagine how I'm going to get you back to the orphanage without going to a lot of trouble. You certainly are a problem.

ANNE. *(Pleading)* Couldn't you possibly let me stay and try to learn to like me? I'd work ever so hard and do everything you told me to—really I would.

MARILLA. *(Firmly)* It's impossible. I won't have a girl in my house.

ANNE. *(Sighing forlornly)* Well, that's another hope gone. My life is a perfect graveyard of buried hopes. That's a sentence I read in a book once, and I say it to comfort myself whenever I'm disappointed in anything. (MATTHEW *enters* C. *from* R., *carrying a newspaper. He has discarded* ANNE'S *hat and her valise. He crosses down to chair* R. *of table* R.C. *and starts to scan his newspaper.)*

MARILLA. *(Irately)* Stuff and nonsense! I don't see where the comforting comes in myself.

ANNE. *(Enthusiastically)* Why, because it sounds so nice and romantic, just as if I were the heroine in a book. I'm so fond of romantic things, and a graveyard full of buried hopes is about as romantic a thing as one can imagine, isn't it? *(Looks directly at the geranium on table* R.C.*)* Oh, what a beautiful geranium. What do you call it?

MARILLA. *(Stiffly)* A geranium, of course. What else could we call it?

ANNE. *(Spiritedly)* But this is such an unusually beautiful geranium that it really ought to have a name. Would you mind awfully if I call it—now let me see—Bonny would do. May I call it Bonny while I'm here? Oh, do let me.

MARILLA. Goodness, I don't care what you call it, but it just doesn't make sense to me.

ANNE. *(Jumping up; gravely)* Oh, but it's most sensible, really it is. How do you know but that it hurts a geranium just to be called that and nothing else? (MATTHEW *looks up from his paper and studies* ANNE.) You wouldn't like to be called nothing but a woman all the time. Yes, I shall call it Bonny.

MARILLA. *(Crossly)* I do wish you'd stop your imaginings and tell me how you came to be in The Hopeton Orphan Asylum.

ANNE. *(Resuming her seat on chair; reluctantly)* Well, you see, both of my parents were terribly in love with each other. They were very poor and had to work terribly hard. They died when I was young and a family by the name of Williams took me in. They knew my parents well.

MATTHEW. *(Thoughtfully)* Williams? Did they have any other children?

ANNE. *(Nodding assent)* Several. And as soon as I was old enough I took care of the children and nursed them when they were sick—all except the oldest boy, Charles. I never took care of him because he was grown up and he worked for a butcher. Don't you think that would be very romantic work? I do. But Charles worried his family terribly.

MARILLA. Why? Didn't he work steadily?

ANNE. Oh, yes, all the time. But one night he failed to come home. It got to be terribly late, so his father went all over town looking for him, but the butcher shop was closed and there was no sign of Charles anywhere. He came home at four o'clock in the morning.

MARILLA. Gracious me! Where had he been?

ANNE. *(Gravely)* Right in the butcher shop. The butcher went home that evening and he told Charles to stay and hang up the meat. So Charles locked the front door and put out the lights and just stayed there all that time.

MARILLA. *(Astonished)* But surely it didn't take him that long to hang up the meat, did it?

ANNE. *(Solemnly)* He said it didn't take him any time at all to hang up the chunks of meat, but he spent hours trying to puzzle out *how to hang up the hamburger! (Settles back in her chair.* MATTHEW *lets out a loud chuckle, rises and laughs heartily.* MARILLA *looks on in displeasure.)*

MARILLA. *(Irately)* Matthew, stop that laughing. The idea! (MATTHEW *stops laughing abruptly and resumes his seat.)* I never heard of anybody hanging up hamburger in all my life. (ANNE *opens her mouth as though to speak but* MARILLA *continues)* If you had a good home with the Williams family, why did you leave there?

ANNE. *(Gravely)* Mrs. Williams passed away and they lost their home and their money. We had a hard time feeding all the children. I never went without food—well, hardly ever, and I always had some kind of clothes, but Mr. Williams thought I'd be better off in an orphanage. *(Looking at* MARILLA *anxiously)* Oh, here I've been talking and I forgot to ask you what you want me to call you. Shall I say Miss Cuthbert? Mayn't I call you Aunt Marilla while I'm here? Then I could imagine that I really belonged to somebody even if it were only for a short time. (MATTHEW *opens his newspaper and starts to read same to himself.)*

MARILLA. *(Stiffly)* No. You'll call me just plain Marilla the same as everybody else does.

ANNE. *(Thoughtfully)* It sounds awfully disrespectful to say just Marilla.

MARILLA. *(Crossly)* Well, I'm not your aunt and I don't believe in calling folks by names that don't belong to them, do you, Matthew?

MATTHEW. *(Looking up from his paper)* Well, I

dunno. Can't say that I do and I can't say that I don't. *(He resumes his reading.)*

ANNE. *(Wistfully)* Couldn't you just imagine that you're my aunt?

MARILLA. *(Stonily)* No, I couldn't. I *never* imagine anything.

ANNE. *(Taking a deep breath; astonished)* Don't you ever? Oh, Miss—oh, Marilla, how much you miss! *(Jumping up)* I've only been here a little while and I've imagined the most wonderful things about this old house. *(Rushes to door R., opens same and looks off R. rapturously)* Oh, what a heavenly garden! Everything out there seems to be calling to me, "Anne, Anne, come out to us. Anne, Anne, we want a playmate!" *(Turning to MARILLA)* Oh, Marilla, please may I go out there just for a little while?

MARILLA. *(Grudgingly)* We-el, I don't suppose that'd do any harm. But mind that you don't leave the garden.

ANNE. *(Enthusiastically)* Oh, thanks so much, Marilla. I believe if I came to know you better I'd like you almost as much as Matthew. You might even come to be a kindred spirit in time. Thanks so much. *(She smiles warmly and exits hastily R. MATTHEW reads his paper intently.)*

MARILLA. *(Terribly upset)* Well, I never saw anything to equal her! This is a pretty kettle of fish. This is what comes of sending word instead of going ourselves. I'll never forgive Nancy Spencer for this—never! Anne will have to be sent back to the asylum. *(Short pause. She looks at MATTHEW angrily)* Matthew Cuthbert, put that paper down and listen to me. Do you hear?

MATTHEW. *(Lowering his newspaper)* What's that, Marilla? Did you say something?

MARILLA. *(Rising; angrily)* I most certainly did.

I said that Anne will have to be sent back to the asylum.

MATTHEW. Yes—er—I suppose so.

MARILLA. *(Taking a few steps* R.*)* You suppose so? Don't you *know?*

MATTHEW. *(Darting a fearful glance at* MARILLA*)* Well, now, she's a real nice little thing. And she's had such a hard life. It's kind of a pity to send her back when she's so set on staying here.

MARILLA. *(Astonished)* Matthew Cuthbert, you don't mean to say you think we ought to keep her?

MATTHEW. *(Nervously)* Well, I dunno. I ain't saying that we ought and I ain't saying that we oughtn't.

MARILLA. *(Angrily)* But what good would she be to us?

MATTHEW. *(In his slow, drawly way)* We-ell, I dunno—but we might be of some good to her.

MARILLA. *(Wrathfully)* I believe that girl has bewitched you, I really do. I can see as plain as plain that you want to keep her here.

MATTHEW. We-el, I ain't saying that I do and I ain't saying that I don't. But anyhow, Marilla, she's a real interesting little thing. Kinda gets under your skin, so she does. You should have heard her talk coming from the station.

MARILLA. *(Angrily)* Oh, she can talk fast enough. I saw that at once. It's nothing in her favor, either. I don't like young folks who have so much to say. I don't want an orphan girl, and if I did she isn't the style I'd pick out.

MATTHEW. *(Summoning all his courage)* I—I could hire young Jerry Buote from down near the creek. He was here the other day asking for a job. And Anne would be company for you, Marilla.

MARILLA. *(Standing* L. *of table* R.C. *and facing him; firmly)* I'm not suffering for company and I'm not going to keep her.

MATTHEW. We-el, now, it's just as you say, of course, Marilla.

MARILLA. Call her in.

MATTHEW. *(Rises and crosses to door R.; opens same and calls off)* Anne! Marilla wants you. *(MARILLA takes over L. to below sofa. MATTHEW retraces his steps to chair R. of table R.C. and sits, resuming his reading of newspaper.)*

ANNE. *(Rushes in R. breathlessly. In her hand are a few flowers)* Oh, Marilla! I had the most gorgeous time. I've named the large cherry tree Snow Queen because it's so white. *(Rushes to C. and comes down to R. of MARILLA, her entire manner changing to one of intense sadness)* You know, Marilla, I really shouldn't have gone out there, after all. It was a tremendous mistake on my part. Now I'll have to leave all the new friends I just made out there.

MARILLA. *(Bewildered)* Friends? But there's nobody in the garden, is there?

ANNE. *(Reproachfully)* Nobody? How can you say that when the garden is filled with flowers and trees and birds? I could stay out there all day just imagining that I'm in an enchanted garden and my oldest sister Gwendolyn is jealous of me because I am beautiful and she is not. Then, just when I am seeing my image in The Lake Of The Shining Water—

MARILLA. *(Breaking in sternly)* Stop that talk. I declare, Anne, I believe your jaw must be hung on a hinge.

ANNE. *(Gravely)* Oh, but it isn't—I can assure you it isn't. It's just that being here and seeing all this beauty fascinates me so that I can't keep my imagination in check.

MARILLA. *(Tartly)* Well, do try to keep your tongue in check.

ANNE. *(Respectfully)* I'll try to remember, Marilla. I wouldn't disobey you for the world. Here are a few flowers I picked for you. I hope you'll like them. *(Offers her the flowers.)*

MARILLA. *(Irritably)* Humph! I don't want the house all cluttered up with flowers. The place for them is in the garden.

ANNE. *(Shyly)* But surely there can't be any harm in having beautiful things in the house, Marilla. Most of us don't have half enough beauty in our lives.

MARILLA. *(Crossly)* Fiddlesticks! Beauty, indeed! You should be thinking of practical things, Anne.

ANNE. *(Sighing forlornly)* Yes, I suppose I should now that I'm so terribly ancient and grown up. You know, Marilla, I don't believe I'll ever realize that I ought to be more dignified and act in a manner becoming to a matronly person, which I am now. It seems like only yesterday that I was playing with my doll, only I never had one because they're too expensive. *(Holding out the flowers to* MARILLA) Do take these, please do. I picked them 'specially for you.

MARILLA. *(Touched in spite of herself but not wishing to show it; crossly)* Oh, well, if I *must* take them, I suppose I must. (MATTHEW *lowers his paper and looks at* MARILLA *with a sly grin on his face.* MARILLA *takes the flowers and faces* ANNE *sternly)* Only, don't think I want them, because I don't. (MATTHEW *emits a loud chuckle.* MARILLA *darts an angry glance at him)* Matthew Cuthbert, stop that laughing. You don't think I actually want these flowers, do you?

MATTHEW. *(Stops laughing abruptly)* We-ll, I dunno. I ain't saying that you do and I ain't saying that you don't.

MARILLA. *(Sternly; to hide her embarrassment)* The idea! I—I'll put the water on for the tea. You must be starved, both of you. *(As she starts for door* L.1, RACHEL *sticks her head in through door* R.*)*

RACHEL. *(Loudly and shrilly)* Did I leave my purse an' parasol here, Marilla? *(Her voice halts* MARILLA, *who pauses and faces her.* ANNE *takes over* L. *a few steps to below sofa.* RACHEL *comes down to* L. *of table* R.C., *sees her purse and parasol and picks them up)* Yes, here they are. I don't know what made me rush off an' leave 'em. *(To* MATTHEW*)* Well, Matthew, where is the little boy you brought back with you?

MATTHEW. *(Rising; nervously)* Why—er—there wasn't any boy—I mean, *he's a girl!*

RACHEL. *(In startled tones)* A girl? But Marilla always said that— *(Pauses abruptly, turns and sees* ANNE *for the first time and surveys her critically)* So you're what they sent instead of a boy, eh? Well, they certainly didn't pick you for your looks, did they?

ANNE. *(Nervously)* Why—er—I—

RACHEL. *(Breaking in quickly and staring at* ANNE*)* My, but she's terribly skinny an' homely, Marilla. Come here, girl, an' lemme have a look at you. Lawful heart, did anybody ever see such freckles? Downright ugly, ain't she? Come here, girl, I say.

ANNE. *(Rushing over to* L. *of* RACHEL *and clenching her fists; loudly and tearfully)* I hate you! D'you hear? I hate you! *(Stamps the floor with her foot)* How dare you call me skinny and ugly? How dare you call attention to my freckles? You are a rude, impolite, unfeeling woman.

MARILLA. *(Stands near door* L.1; *excitedly)* Anne, stop that this instant.

ANNE. *(Her voice vibrating with anger as she faces* RACHEL*)* How dare you say such things about me? How would you like to have me tell you that you're clumsy and haven't a spark of imagination in you? I hate you, d'you hear, you—you gimlet eye! *(Rushes up to door L.2, sobbing loudly, and exits.)*

RACHEL. *(Completely horrified)* Well, I must say! Well, did anybody ever see such a temper? I don't envy you your job bringin' up that girl, Marilla.

MARILLA. I'm not bringing her up, Rachel. She's going back tomorrow. But you shouldn't have twitted her about her looks. Nobody likes to be told that they're homely. (MARILLA *exits hastily* L.I.)

RACHEL. *(Turning to* MATTHEW *angrily)* I never dreamed Marilla would uphold a girl who displayed such a vi'lent temper, did you, Matthew?

MATTHEW. *(Coldly)* We-el, I ain't saying that I have and I ain't saying that I haven't.

RACHEL. *(Wrathfully)* I'm goin' in an' tell Marilla Cuthbert a few things, so I am. If she had asked *my* advice this never would o' happened. *(Crosses to door L.I and exits.)*

MATTHEW. *(Goes up to door L.2, opens same and calls off softly)* Anne. Come on out. I'm here alone. Come out, Anne. *(Retraces his steps to C.)*

ANNE. *(Enters L.2 slowly and rubbing her eyes as though trying to hold the tears back)* Oh, Matthew, I'm the saddest girl in the world. *(Comes down to L. of* MATTHEW*)* That dreadful woman did terrible things to me. I'd just convinced myself after months of imagining that my freckles are beauty marks, and she spoiled it all. I'll never be happy again.

MATTHEW. *(Angrily)* Rachel Lynde is a meddlesome gossip. But it's too bad it had to happen just now, because I was trying to coax Marilla to let you stay here at least for awhile.

ANNE. *(Wistfully)* Oh, Matthew, were you really? Oh, how I'd love it if she'd only let me. I'd do *anything* if you could make Marilla change her mind and let me stay—*anything*.

MATTHEW. Would you apologize to Rachel Lynde and tell her you're sorry you lost your temper just now?

ANNE. *(Hesitating)* Why—I don't know. It would be terribly difficult. Perhaps I might get around it by imagining I'm sorry. *(Eagerly)* Do you think Marilla might let me stay if I apologize?

MATTHEW. *(Uncertainly)* We-el, I dunno. I ain't saying that she will and I ain't saying that she won't. But it would be a help.

ANNE. *(Resolutely)* Then I'll do it. If you really want me to, Matthew. I never could refuse you anything.

MATTHEW. *(Cautiously)* Only you mustn't tell Marilla that I suggested it. She might think I was putting my oar in, and that would make her angry.

ANNE. *(Firmly)* Wild horses won't drag the secret from me. How would wild horses drag a secret from a person, anyhow?

MARILLA. *(Outside of door L.1)* I don't want anything more said about it, Rachel. (MATTHEW *places a finger to his lips warningly and crosses over to* R. *of table* R.C. ANNE *stands just* L. *of table* R.C.)

RACHEL. *(As she enters L.1)* Well, I'll never put a foot inside this house again 'til that girl apologizes to me. *(Crosses* R. *to below sofa.* MARILLA *enters* L.1 *and stands in front of door.)*

ANNE. *(Nervously)* Marilla, I—I—

MARILLA. *(Breaking in sternly)* You've heard what Mrs. Lynde said, Anne. I think she's within her rights, and I expect you to ask her to forgive you.   *(WARN Curtain.)*

ANNE. *(Turning to* RACHEL *and taking a deep breath as though preparing for a most unpleasant task)* Oh, Mrs. Lynde, I'm so extremely sorry. I could never express my sorrow, no, not if I used up the whole dictionary. I behaved terribly to you and I disgraced dear Matthew and poor Marilla.

MARILLA. *(Nodding assent)* That's better, Anne. Now, I'm sure it will be best never to refer to this matter again.

ANNE. *(Eagerly)* Oh, but I've only just started to apologize, Marilla. *(Facing RACHEL again; eloquently)* It was wicked of me to fly into a rage just because you told me the truth—it was the truth, every word you said to me. I am freckeled and ugly and skinny. Oh, Mrs. Lynde, please, please forgive me. If you refuse it will be a lifelong sorrow to me. Please say you forgive me, Mrs. Lynde, please do.

RACHEL. *(With an air of great condescension; stiffly)* You've been a very naughty girl, but considerin' that you're just a poor orphan an' ain't had no bringin' up, I s'pose I'll hafta forgive you.

ANNE. *(Delightedly)* Oh, thank you, Mrs. Lynde. It's so sweet of you. It shows you have a kind heart after all. *(Crosses to R. of RACHEL and extends her hand.)*

RACHEL. *(Taking her hand half-heartedly)* Well, I hope this will teach you to hold onto your temper, Anne.

ANNE. *(Gravely)* I certainly hope so. (RACHEL *drops* ANNE'S *hand.* ANNE, *with wide-eyed innocence)* Of course, everything I said about you was true, but I shouldn't have said it! (RACHEL *emits a scream of anger.* MATTHEW *bursts into hearty laughter.* MARILLA *glares at* MATTHEW *angrily.* ANNE *looks on innocently as the Curtain falls swiftly.)*

END OF ACT ONE

ACT TWO

SCENE: *Same as previous scene.*

TIME: *The following September; afternoon.*
LIGHTS outside of screen door R. *to denote bright sunlight. All LIGHTS on stage full up.*

DISCOVERED AT RISE: MARILLA *sits on rocking chair up* L., *busily engaged at her knitting. She wears a severely plain taffeta dress of a dark color, the silk so stiff that it could stand alone. The dress is made along old-fashioned lines. It is obvious that she is dressed for a special occasion. The instant the Curtain rises the DOORBELL jangles off* R. MARILLA *rises, crosses to arch and exits* C. *to* R.

MARILLA. *(Off up* R.; *cordially)* Well, I do declare if it isn't Mrs. Barry. Come right in, won't you? We haven't seen you in weeks. *(Re-enters* C. *from* R., *followed by* MRS. BARRY, *who is smartly dressed in a linen or cloth coat suit, a becoming hat, gloves, purse, etc.* MARILLA *comes to below sofa.)*

MRS. BARRY. *(Following to below chair* L. *of table* R.C.*)* I've been so busy getting Diana ready for school and shopping for myself that I haven't had any time for visiting. *(Sitting on chair* L. *of table and removing her gloves)* It seems as though there's always something to attend to.

MARILLA. *(Sitting on sofa; severely)* It's the same with me. I never get a chance to set any more.

57

Now that Anne is here it seems like I just go from one thing to the other.

MRS. BARRY. *(Knowingly)* I imagined that she'd keep you busy.

MARILLA. *(Witheringly)* Busy? Seems like I spend my life picking up after her.

MRS. BARRY. She's brought a great change to my home, too. Diana isn't the same girl since Anne took up her abode here. I never saw two girls who cared more deeply for each other right from the start.

MARILLA. *(Crossly)* That's all I hear from morning to night. Diana this and Diana that. Yesterday Diana and she were sea-gulls. There's no telling what they'll be today.

MRS. BARRY. *(Smiling)* At least it has kept Diana outdoors, and that's been extremely beneficial to her. She and Anne share the same desk at school and Diana claims that Anne is the smartest girl in the class.

MARILLA. *(Severely)* I'll wager she talks more than the whole class put together. But her teacher told me at church that Anne is considerable bright.

MRS. BARRY. I never saw anybody who was so eager to make friends. Anne has a positive genius for friendship.

MARILLA. *(Stiffly)* She has a genius for making mistakes and for using big words. Half the time I don't know what she's talking about.

MRS. BARRY. *(Laughingly)* You should follow Anne's example and draw on your imagination. *(Curiously)* Are you going to keep her with you permanently?

MARILLA. *(Undecided)* Well, I can't say that I am and I can't say that I'm not. *(Astonished)* Sakes alive, if I'm not talking just like Matthew. It's all his doings that Anne's still here. I've got nothing to do with it.

MRS. BARRY. Matthew urged you to keep Anne? But of course if you hadn't wanted her here—

MARILLA. *(Breaking in quickly)* I've never wanted her. But Matthew is so exasperating. He pointed out that there's no sense in being a church member if a body ain't going to act in a Christian manner. It was a case of keeping her or sending her back to the orphanage, and she cried and pleaded so hard to stay and Matthew is so taken with the idea—

MRS. BARRY. *(Interrupting her with a knowing air)* You needn't make all those apologies to me, my dear. I actually believe that you're learning to care for Anne yourself.

MARILLA. *(Jumping up and facing* MRS. BARRY; *irately)* How can you even think such a thing? I've never brought up a child and I'll probably make a mess of it, but I'm only doing it to please Matthew.

MRS. BARRY. *(Apologetically)* Forgive me for saying that. I was wrong—*apparently. (Stresses the last word)* But it might be that you'll learn to love Anne before she's here much longer.

MARILLA. *(Severely)* Fiddlesticks! I don't believe in such carryings on. I try to take an interest in the girl because an old maid knows more about raising a girl than an old bachelor like Matthew. *(Resumes her seat on sofa and attacks her knitting vigorously)* It's the most surprising thing to me that my brother should be so set on keeping Anne here when he's always dreaded little girls so.

MRS. BARRY. It is amazing, isn't it? From what Diana tells me, Anne rushes to Matthew with all her troubles and tells him everything she does.

MARILLA. *(Jealously)* She don't run to him any more than she does to me. And she certainly tells me everything. It ain't in her to keep anything to herself. She's never happy unless she's talking.

MRS. BARRY. *(Curiously)* Does Mrs. Rachel come over as much as she formerly did?

MARILLA. Oh, yes, more's the pity. Anne spent an entire hour apologizing to her, but do you know, Mrs. Barry, I was sort of glad she spoke to Rachel as she did.

MRS. BARRY. *(Nodding assent)* So was I. We laughed for hours at what Anne said to her when she apologized. *(Laughs lightly.)*

MARILLA. *(Grudgingly)* For all of her temper and her constant gabbing, I must say that Anne ain't deceitful or sly. And there ain't a stingy bone in her body. She'd share anything she has with whoever happens to be with her.

MRS. BARRY. She's forever picking flowers for Diana, and if she has two caramels she'd never consider eating both of them. One has to be saved for her Diana.

MARILLA. *(Stiffly)* She'd carry half this house over to yours if I'd let her. *(Sighing dismally)* I don't know how to cure her of being so outspoken. You know I made three new dresses for her. She didn't have anything fit to wear.

MRS. BARRY. *(Bewildered)* Wasn't she grateful to you for making them?

MARILLA. *(Tartly)* Humph! She said she'd have to try to *imagine* she liked them.

MRS. BARRY. *(Bewildered)* What?

MARILLA. *(Nodding assent)* She just couldn't take to the dresses 'cause they weren't pretty and didn't have puffed sleeves. Seems that all of her life Anne has longed for a white dress with puffed sleeves. She'd look pretty traipsing to school in that kind of a outfit, wouldn't she?

MRS. BARRY. *(Smiling)* Oh, well, she's only a child. Between you and your brother I'm sure Anne will turn out to be a great success.

MARILLA. *(Sternly)* Matthew ain't to have nothing to do with her upbringing. He's given me his word as to that. I wouldn't have allowed Anne to stay under this roof unless her raising was left entirely to me.

MRS. BARRY. *(Firmly)* Of course, you have the consolation of knowing that you can always send Anne back to the orphanage if she becomes too much of a responsibility. *(Looks up at* MARILLA *out of the corner of her eye without turning her head.)*

MARILLA. And admit that I've been a failure? No, sir-ee. *(Resolutely)* When I tackle a thing I aim to see it through. I'm no quitter. And I'm going to make Anne into a well-mannered girl, come what may.

MRS. BARRY. *(Smiling in a knowing manner)* It's just as I thought.

MARILLA. *(Rising; suspiciously)* Huh? What's that? What do you mean?

MRS. BARRY. *(Rising)* Oh, never mind. I'll tell you some other time. But I have opinions of my own as to why you are keeping Anne here and I'm *not* using my imagination.

MARILLA. *(Bewildered)* I don't understand you nohow.

MRS. BARRY. *(Putting on her gloves as she crosses up to arch)* Diana was so anxious to get to school today. It seems that that wealthy Blythe boy is back in Avonlea and will attend school today for the first time this season.

MARILLA. *(Crossing up to* L. *of* MRS. BARRY*)* I'll hear all about that from Anne when she comes home—and more, too. For the past few weeks, all I've been listening to is plans for the Sunday School picnic tomorrow.

MRS. BARRY. *(Smiling)* I've had to listen to my share of that, too. It's Anne's first picnic, so it's easy to understand why she's so enthusiastic about it. *(Wistfully)* It's so wonderful to be young and have all of one's illusions before one.

MARILLA. *(Severely)* Humph! I don't believe in any of that foolishness. Young or old, we all have our work to do in this world, share and share alike.

MRS. BARRY. *(Thoughtfully)* But we must season that with a little pleasure. I'm sure you'd be rewarded for all of your trouble with Anne if you could hear some of the lovely things she says about you.

MARILLA. *(Taken off her guard; agog with curiosity)* Does she? What does she say? *(Clearing her throat hastily and resuming her severe manner)* Never mind. Don't tell me. I'd be a lot better pleased if Anne would keep her mind on what I tell her to do and do it the first time I ask her to instead of talking so much that she makes me forget what I've asked her to do.

MRS. BARRY. *(With a broad smile)* Cheer up and try to be patient. I have my troubles with Diana, too, even though she is my own child. Do try to come over. We must see each other more often now that Anne and Diana are such close friends. *(Exits C. to R.)*

MARILLA. I'll go to the front door with you. *(Exits C. to R. after MRS. BARRY. ANNE sticks her head in through door R. and looks around cautiously. Seeing that the room is empty, she enters. In one hand she carries a slate, a few school books and a pen and pencil box, all strapped together. In the other hand is a handkerchief with which she dabs at her eyes, trying to wipe away the tears that persist in coming. She wears the same sailor hat but her dress is of a better material than in previous scene. It is newer, but the sleeves are decidedly plain, as is the entire dress. She crosses to C., then hears MARILLA exclaim off R. loudly, "Goodbye. Come again soon." ANNE looks around quickly, rushes up to door* L.2, *emits a soft sob and exits quickly, closing the door after her.* MARILLA *enters* C. *from* R., *followed by* MATTHEW. *The latter wears a pair of nondescript trousers, a soft blue working shirt, no necktie, a vest that is a different color than his trousers and a wide-brimmed hat of straw that has seen better days.)*

MATTHEW. *(Removing his hat as he enters)* Warm for this time of the year, ain't it, Marilla? *(Comes down* R. *and sits* R. *of table* R.C.*)*

MARILLA. *(Coming down to sofa and sitting)* I've been too busy to notice. Seems like I'm on the go all the time lately.

MATTHEW. I've been working pretty hard myself in the fields.

MARILLA. *(Incredulously)* You don't think your work is as hard or as tiring as *my* work is, do you?

MATTHEW. *(Tactfully)* We-el, I dunno. I ain't saying that it is and I ain't saying that it ain't.

MARILLA. *(Severely)* When you finish in the evening you're all through, but housework is never finished. *(Looking up at him curiously)* Where've you been, Matthew? Didn't you have a package in your hand when you came in?

MATTHEW. *(In his drawly manner)* We-el, I ain't saying that I had and I ain't saying that I hadn't.

MARILLA. *(Rising and pointing a finger at him accusingly)* You've been to town again and bought something else for Anne.

MATTHEW. *(Uncomfortably)* We-el, now, I ain't.

MARILLA. *(Breaking in quickly)* Matthew Cuthbert, you'll spoil that girl beyond all reason. I declare that you think more of her than anybody in this world. If Anne took a notion to get up in the middle of the night and have dinner, you'd say it was all right. *(Resumes her seat on sofa and attacks her knitting industriously.)*

MATTHEW. I ain't saying that I would and I ain't saying that I wouldn't. But you've gotta admit, Marilla, that Anne is obedient and she does try to please.

MARILLA. *(Knitting swiftly; sourly)* She don't have to try to please you, Matthew. And as for her being obedient, I'd expect that of any child I took to raise.

MATTHEW. *(Proudly)* We-el, you gotta admit, then, that Anne has improved a lot in the short time she's been here.

MARILLA. *(Frowning)* Improved? How?

MATTHEW. She ain't lost her temper once since that day she turned on Rachel Lynde, and she ain't called anybody "gimlet-eye" since that day.

MARILLA. *(Severely)* I shouldn't think she would. Of course, it didn't matter so much with Rachel, but it was the principle of the thing. Anne has promised me not to ever lose her temper again.

MATTHEW. *(Proudly)* And that's one promise she'll keep, too. I know Anne.

MARILLA. *(Facing him; astonished)* Since when have you been such a judge of girls, Matthew Cuthbert? It's the first time I ever heard you express an opinion about one of them.

MATTHEW. *(Uncomfortably)* We-el, I ain't saying that I know anything about girls and I ain't saying that I don't. I'm just saying that I do know a lot about Anne. (RACHEL *sticks her head in through door* R.)

MARILLA. *(Turning and seeing* RACHEL; *irately)* Do come in and close that screen door, Rachel. You'll let in all the flies.

RACHEL. *(Enters and crosses to* C. *She is dressed much the same as in previous Act but is without a hat, purse or umbrella)* I just thought I'd run in from next door to tell you the news. Who d'you s'pose is back in Avonlea? *(Comes down to chair L. of table R.C. and sits.)*

MARILLA. Who?

RACHEL. *(Excitedly)* Mr. Blythe and his son, Gilbert.

MARILLA. *(Lightly)* Oh, I know all about that. Gilbert Blythe is in Anne's class at school.

RACHEL. They say it's a caution the way he teased all the girls last year.

MARILLA. I used to know his father when I was real young. I always thought he was most pleasant.

RACHEL. *(Stiffly)* Well, I never have had any time for him. He's too uppity, if you ask me.

MARILLA. *(Firmly)* He never was uppity with me.

RACHEL. *(With an indignant toss of her head)* Oh, you like him because he proba'ly told you you looked like a rosebud back in eighteen hundred an' eighty.

MARILLA. *(Dropping her knitting; wrathfully)* I wasn't alive in eighteen hundred and eighty, was I, Matthew?

MATTHEW. *(As though thinking of other things)* Huh? What's that, Marilla?

MARILLA. *(Firmly)* I said I wasn't alive in eighteen hundred and eighty, was I?

MATTHEW. *(Fingering his chin reflectively)* Well, I dunno. Can't say that you were and I can't say that you weren't.

MARILLA. *(Jumping up angrily)* What?

MATTHEW. *(Weakly)* Why—er—you know, Marilla, I never was very good at remembering dates.

MARILLA. *(Resuming her seat on sofa)* Well, I wasn't, so there. I could prove it by showing the family Bible if I wanted to.

RACHEL. *(Eagerly)* Could you, Marilla? Then get it out. I've always wanted to see it.

MARILLA. *(Resuming her knitting; hastily)* Some

otl .er time. I've got too much to attend to right now. (MATTHEW *rises.*) Matthew, did Moody Spurgeon come to take Dimples away?

MATTHEW. Reckon he did, 'cause she ain't out in the barn and she was there 'fore I drove to town.

RACHEL. *(Eagerly)* Who's Dimples? I ain't never heard you mention her before.

MARILLA. Well, if you must know, she's one of our pigs. Anne named her "Dimples" because she's so full of them.

RACHEL. *(Scornfully)* Mercy days, what next? Callin' a pig "Dimples." I ain't never heard tell o' such nonsense.

MARILLA. Mind that you get the money for her, Matthew. Moody must have taken her home while you were away.

RACHEL. *(Turning to* MATTHEW; *eagerly)* If I'd o' known you were sellin' a pig I might o' bought it for us. How much did you get for her, Matthew? Did she bring you much?

MATTHEW. *(Reflectively)* We-el, I dunno. I ain't got it yet. *(As he crosses to* R. *door)* Don't know as you'd call it much and I don't know as you wouldn't. It all depends on what you mean by much. *(Exits hastily.)*

RACHEL. *(Turning and facing* MARILLA; *irritably)* I declare that Matthew is the most irritatin' man I've ever met. A body never can get a thing outa him.

MARILLA. *(Gleefully)* He always tells me what I want to know, Rachel. You just don't know how to handle him.

RACHEL. *(Spitefully)* You musta learned just recent, then. *(Eyeing* MARILLA *intently)* Great day in the mornin' if you ain't got on your best go-to-meetin' dress. What's happenin' today, Marilla?

MARILLA. *(Impatiently)* Well, if you must know,

the new Minister's wife, Mrs. Allan, is coming here
to tea this afternoon.

RACHEL. *(Visibly disappointed)* Oh, is that all?
She was to my house last week. I thought it'd be
somethin' important.

MARILLA. *(Proudly)* It's important to Anne.
She's taken such a fancy to Mrs. Allan that she
begged to have permission to invite her here, and
when I said she might she got up at six this morning to bake a special layer cake for her guest.

RACHEL. *(Stiffly)* If you ask me, I don't set so
much store by the new Minister's wife. For one
thing she's too worldly. She's apt to put foolish
notions into Anne's head. If you'd asked *my* advice,
but o' course you didn't, I'd have made Anne stay
in school this afternoon.

MARILLA. *(Bewildered)* Stay in school? But
Anne is at school. She hardly ate any lunch she was
so busy fussing with her layer cake, and then she
rushed right out so as to be on time for the afternoon session.

RACHEL. *(As though exploding a bomb)* I said
Anne ain't at school an' I reckon I know what I'm
talkin' 'bout. That girl has too much freedom. Mark
my words, Marilla Cuthbert, she'll come to a bad
end.

MARILLA. *(Dropping her knitting on sofa and
rising quickly)* But if Anne ain't at school, where
is she?

RACHEL. I don't know. I ain't had time to find
out. But I mean to try, an' when I do I'll come right
back an' let you know.

(JOSIE PYE, *a tall, gangling girl of fifteen, enters* R.
*She is at that awkward age when she appears
to be even gawkier than she really is. She giggles constantly and tries to assume a most superior manner. She is at her best when relating*

*a choice piece of gossip. Wears a gingham
dress that has wide puffed sleeves and a patent
leather belt at the waist. Her hair hangs in one
long braid down her back and is tied with a
ribbon.)*

JOSIE. *(As she enters)* Mister Matthew told me
I could come in this way. Is Anne home yet? *(Giggles and crosses to* C. MARILLA *stands just below
sofa.* RACHEL *stands below chair* L. *of table* R.C.*)*
Tell her I gotta message for her, please, Miss Marilla.

MARILLA. Anne's not home from school yet,
Josie.

JOSIE. *(Firmly)* Oh, but she must be. She run
outa school hours ago.

RACHEL. *(Triumphantly)* There! Didn't I tell
you, Marilla? Reckon you'll pay some attention to
what I tell you after this. *(Crossing to* R. *of* JOSIE;
commanding) What went on at school this afternoon, Josie?

JOSIE. *(Giggling and hanging her head)* Oh, I
couldn't tell you. It was *too* awful. Gosh, it was
more fun than a barrel o' monkeys.

MARILLA. *(Crossing up to* L. *of* JOSIE; *commanding)* Josie Pye, if you don't tell me this instant what
Anne did at school, I'll take you home to your
mother and get her to make you tell me.

JOSIE. *(Fearfully)* Oh, don't do that, Miss Marilla. I'll tell you, only it's so awful you won't ever
believe it in a million years. Gosh, some fun! *(Giggles.)*

RACHEL. *(In a frenzy of impatience)* Well, come
on—out with it. Tell us everythin' just as it happened.

JOSIE. *(Taking a deep breath)* Well, you know I
sit right behind Anne an' Diana. That Gilbert
Blythe sits just across the way from us. This morn-

in' I heard Anne say to Diana, "Well, I admit your Gilbert Blythe is han'some, but I think he's very bold. He ac'chually winked at me just now, an' that's not good manners!" *(Giggles)* Gosh, some fun!

MARILLA. *(Severely)* Are you going to tell us about this afternoon or aren't you?

JOSIE. *(Remonstrating)* I'm tellin' you right now. This afternoon Anne was sittin' at her desk readin' —my, but she's the readin'est girl what I've ever seen—an' Gilbert Blythe leaned over an' whispered right at Anne loud enuff for us all to hear, "Freckles! Freckles!" Just like that.

MARILLA. *(Fearfully)* Oh, he didn't. How awful.

JOSIE. *(Firmly)* He sure did. I was right there an' heard him. *(Giggles)* Gosh, some fun!

RACHEL. *(Disappointed)* Was that all that there was to it?

JOSIE. *(Spiritedly)* 'Deed it wasn't. That was just the start. Anne didn't pay no mind to him at first, so he leaned over closer to her an' whispered: "I could do the multiplication tables by countin' your freckles— Freckles!" Then he just grinned as hard as he could.

MARILLA. *(Wailing)* Oh, dear!

JOSIE. *(Enjoying herself hugely)* Anne just jumped outa her seat an' stood aside Gilbert an' shouted right out loud, "You mean, hateful boy! How dare you?"

RACHEL. *(Excited)* What?

JOSIE. *(Spiritedly)* An' then she upped with a slate, brought it down on Gilbert's head an' cracked it clear across.

MARILLA. *(Moaningly)* Cracked his head?

JOSIE. No, the slate. An' you ain't heard the worst yet, neither. *(Giggles)* Gosh, some fun!

RACHEL. *(Elated)* I don't see what she could have done that'd be worse.

JOSIE. *(Firmly)* I'll tell you what. She didn't hit Gilbert over the head with her own slate. It belonged to Diana an' now you'll hafta buy Diana Barry a new slate, Miss Marilla.

MARILLA. *(Groaning)* Oh, this is dreadful! *(Crosses down to below sofa.)*

RACHEL. *(In her best "I told you so" manner)* You never should have taken her in in the first place, Marilla. I tried to warn you but you wouldn't listen. *(Rushing over to door R.)* I won't say a word 'bout this to anybody, but I s'pose by this time everybody in town knows it. *(Exits quickly R.)*

MARILLA. *(Anxiously)* Did Anne leave school right after she brought the slate down on Gilbert's head?

JOSIE. *(Shaking her head "no")* No, indeedy. Our teacher called Anne up front, an' he told her she had the worst temper he ever saw. *(Giggles.* ANNE *emerges through door* L.2, *unobserved by the* OTHERS. *She has discarded her hat and her books but still carries her handkerchief.)* Then he wrote on the blackboard for the whole class to see: "Ann Shirley has a very bad temper. Ann Shirley must learn to control her temper."

ANNE. *(Tearfully)* I wouldn't have minded that so much if he only hadn't spelled my name without an "e."

MARILLA. *(Turning and facing* ANNE *and placing both hands on her hips)* Anne, I'm ashamed of you. Where have you been since you left school? Why didn't you come directly to me and tell me about it?

ANNE. *(Coming over to* L. *of* MARILLA; *tearfully)* Because I knew some tattle-tale like Josie Pye would get here first, and I've been thinking of ways and means of removing myself from this vale of tears and sorrows. (MARILLA *stands* C. JOSIE *is* R. *of her,* ANNE *is* L. *of her.)*

JOSIE. *(Before* MARILLA *has a chance to speak)*

I ain't a tattle-tale, Anne Shirley. I came here to deliver a message from Gilbert Blythe. He asked me to.

ANNE. *(Angrily)* Don't you ever dare mention his name to me again. Anybody who does is my enemy for the rest of my existence, which, from present indications, promises to be brief, indeed.

MARILLA. *(Crossing down to below sofa L.C.)* Anne, you come here to me.

ANNE. *(To JOSIE; spiritedly)* Now if you're satisfied you can go home and tell everybody that I'm never going back to school again.

JOSIE. *(Astonished)* You ain't? Not ever?

ANNE. *(Resolutely)* I said never—that means permanent.

JOSIE. *(Rushes R. to door)* I'll hafta tell Gilbert you wouldn't lissen to his message. Oh, gosh, some fun! *(Giggles and exits hastily.)*

ANNE. *(Coming down to R. of sofa; thoughtfully)* You know, Marilla, when I first came here I wished so hard that I had been born a boy, but since I've seen Gil—I mean, a certain boy, I'm glad I'm a girl and that I'm not his sister. *(Sinks onto the hassock below sofa and buries her eyes in her handkerchief, sobbing softly.)*

MARILLA. *(Severely)* Well, I must say, Anne, that your behavior is disgraceful. First you insult Mrs. Lynde, now it's Gilbert Blythe, and—

ANNE. *(Breaking in hastily)* It's Matthew I'm thinking of. I promised him I'd never lose my temper again. *(Removing her handkerchief from her eyes and looking up at MARILLA anxiously)* Marilla, which d'you suppose is the quickest and most painful way of taking one's self out of this world and into the next?

MARILLA. *(Sternly)* Anne Shirley, don't you ever dare even think of such a thing.

ANNE. *(Tearfully)* Everything was getting along

so beautifully, even if I did put the pie in the oven yesterday and forget to take it out until it had burned to a crisp. I felt that I was making fewer mistakes each day and I was so proud of being "Anne of Green Gables" and now—now I had to go and lose my temper without even knowing that I was losing it. *(She sobs loudly and applies her handkerchief again.* MATTHEW *enters* R., *followed by* GILBERT BLYTHE, *a manly and fine-looking boy of about sixteen.* GILBERT *is possessed of an extremely attractive personality, and in spite of the fact that he is all boy and enjoys playing pranks, he is sincere and refined in manner, intelligent and of good breeding. He wears a pair of grey flannel slacks, soft shirt with collar attached, bright necktie, a sport jacket of a contrasting color, brown sport shoes; no hat.)*

MARILLA. *(Sternly)* You'll have to be punished severely for this, Anne.

GILBERT. *(Coming down* C. *to* R. *of sofa; apologetically)* Please, Miss Cuthbert, may I say a few words? (MARILLA *and* ANNE *jump up quickly.* MATTHEW *crosses up and exits* C. *to* R.)

ANNE. *(She takes over to* L. *of sofa and faces* GILBERT *angrily)* Gilbert Blythe, how dared you come inside this house? You've ruined my entire life. Aren't you satisfied with that?

MARILLA. *(Irately)* Anne, hold your tongue.

GILBERT. *(To* MARILLA*)* I tried to apologize to Anne but she wouldn't give me a chance. I admit that it was all my fault. I'd no business to tease her so in the first place.

ANNE. *(Angrily)* Go away, go away.

GILBERT. *(Pleading with* ANNE*)* You aren't going to be bad friends with me forever just because of this, are you? I'll promise never to mention your freckles again if you'll forgive me.

ANNE. *(With great dignity)* What you ask is

impossible. If I decide to go on living, there are two pathways before me, and the one that leads far away from you is the one I must take.

MARILLA. *(To* ANNE; *astonished)* Anne, wherever did you make up such a speech from?

ANNE. *(The great lady; holding herself very erect)* I prefer not to *indulge* the source of my speech until we are alone, Marilla.

GILBERT. *(Grinning broadly)* You mean divulge, Anne.

ANNE. *(Regally)* Is the gentleman speaking to you, Marilla? Because I'm not at all interested in anything he has to say.

GILBERT. *(Gravely)* Well, I suppose if she won't forgive me and be friends, there isn't anything more I can do about it, Miss Cuthbert. But I hope you won't punish Anne. She doesn't deserve it—really she doesn't.

ANNE. *(To* MARILLA; *haughtily)* Please inform Mr. Blythe for Miss Shirley that he needn't worry about any punishment that may be meted out to her. The worst punishment that could happen to her is having to be in the same room with him. *(Crosses up and exits quickly* L.2.*)*

GILBERT. *(Disconsolately)* There doesn't seem to be much hope that she'll change her mind, does there? *(Admiringly)* She surely has a lot of spirit.

MARILLA. *(Tersely)* She has that, all right. And a lot of temper along with it.

GILBERT. *(Rubbing the top of his head painfully)* Don't I know it?

MARILLA. She's terribly sensitive about her freckles. The mention of them gets her so riled—

GILBERT. *(Breaking in hastily)* This has taught me a lesson. I'll never tease another girl no matter how badly I want to.

MATTHEW. *(Enters* C. *from* R., *carrying a small package wrapped in paper and neatly tied)* Any luck, Son? *(Comes down to* R. *of* GILBERT *and smiles at him.)*

GILBERT. *(Shaking his head "no")* Not so far, sir. (ANNE *sticks her head through door* L.2, *sees* GILBERT *and withdraws her head quickly, closing the door with a bang.)* Perhaps Anne will change her mind in a few days and forgive me. *(To* MARILLA*)* Promise me that you won't punish her. That will make me feel better.

MARILLA. *(Hesitating)* We-el, we'll see.

GILBERT. *(Turning to* MATTHEW*)* You won't try to inflict punishment on Anne, will you, sir?

MARILLA. *(Severely)* Humph! He ain't got anything to do with raising Anne. She's my problem. (MATTHEW *winks at* GILBERT *in a knowing manner and turns away.)*

GILBERT. *(To* MARILLA; *politely)* Oh, I see. Well, I'm mighty sorry this happened and that my first visit here was on such an unpleasant mission. May I come again?

MARILLA. *(Cordially)* Of course. I'm sure Anne will be sorry she snubbed you and be willing to be friendly in a few days.

GILBERT. *(Eagerly)* You do? That's fine. I feel better now. Thanks so much, both of you. 'Bye. *(Crosses up and exits* C. *to* R.*)*

MARILLA. *(Crossing to* L. *of* MATTHEW*)* Nice, polite boy, ain't he? Seems terribly anxious to be friends with Anne. She claims she won't go back to school. We'll have to talk her out of that, Matthew.

MATTHEW. *(Grinning broadly)* You mean *you'll* have to do it. Remember that *you're* the one what's raising her.

MARILLA. *(Agog with curiosity)* Matthew Cuthbert, that's the package you had when you came in from town awhile ago. Who's it for?

MATTHEW. We-el, I ain't saying that it's for anybody and then again I ain't saying that it ain't.

MARILLA. *(Turning away from him; stiffly)* I'm not interested in your old package anyhow. *(Crosses to sofa L.C. and resumes her seat.)*

MATTHEW. *(Crossing to R. of sofa)* Reckon you'd be interested if you knew what was in it. Wouldn't you just?

MARILLA. *(Stiffly)* Humph! You're just trying to get me stirred up about it, and I won't be stirred. *(Turning to him eagerly)* Well, what *is* in it?

MATTHEW. *(Handing her the package)* It's for you. Open it up and see how you like it.

MARILLA. *(Taking the package and opening it with great haste)* For me? Lands sakes! *(Holds up a lovely white lace collar)* Well, Matthew Cuthbert, whatever possessed you to buy me such an expensive collar?

MATTHEW. I didn't buy it for you, Marilla. It's from Anne.

MARILLA. *(Bewildered)* From Anne? *(Rising and examining the collar)* Where did she get the money?

MATTHEW. She's been helping me with the berrying and I paid her so much a pail. She saved all her money to buy that collar for you.

MARILLA. *(Softening perceptibly)* Well, that was real thoughtful of her, I must say. (MATTHEW *grins in a knowing manner.* MARILLA *looks up at him and resumes her former severe manner)* Not that I side in with such woeful waste. She might better have saved her money.

MATTHEW. *(Knowingly)* Now, Marilla, you know that deep down in your heart you appreciate Anne's thinking of you.

MARILLA. *(Gruffly, to hide her embarrassment)* Who said I didn't appreciate it? But you know I never was one for wearing fol-der-ols.

MATTHEW. *(Crossing to chair L. of table R.C. and sitting)* No, nor for showing your real feelings, either.

ANNE. *(Sticking her head in through door* L2 *and glancing around the room anxiously)* Has that Gil—I mean, has that certain boy gone, Matthew? (MATTHEW *turns and faces her and nods reassuringly.)* Well, that's something to be thankful for on this thankless day. *(Enters and comes down to* L. *of sofa.)*

MARILLA. *(Grudgingly)* I want to thank you for this collar, Anne. It's real pert. Never thought Matthew had the good taste to pick out such a nice collar.

ANNE. Oh, Matthew didn't pick it out. I did—the last time he drove me to town. But I couldn't get it until today because I didn't have all the money. Matthew wanted to advance it to me, but considering how uncertain life is at best, I decided to wait until I had all of the money saved. I do hope you like it, Marilla.

MARILLA. *(Stiffly)* I like it, Anne, but I'm not going to make this collar blind me to my duty. (MATTHEW *clears his throat.)* Gilbert Blythe had no right to tease you, but you shouldn't have lost your temper and created a scene in school.

ANNE. *(Dropping onto hassock below sofa; sadly)* The stars in their courses are against me, Marilla. Of course, what happened to me today was simply tragical, and no matter how long I live I'll never be able to erase the memory of what Gil—I mean, a certain boy said about my freckles. But I don't suppose it matters so much because I'm never going back to that school while Mr. Phillips is the teacher there.

MARILLA. *(Turning to* MATTHEW *angrily)* You hear that, Matthew? What have you to say to it?

MATTHEW. *(Reflectively)* We-el, I dunno as I've anything to say, Marilla, and then again I don't know but what I have. Anne is in your charge and

I ain't got a thing to do with her raising. *(He darts
a triumphant glance at* MARILLA.*)*

MARILLA. *(Irritably)* Really, Matthew Cuthbert,
there are times when I wish you'd grow up and
show some sense.

ANNE. *(Loyally)* Matthew is very grown up, Marilla. And he has more sense than any man I've
ever met. He uses his brains for other things than
headaches.

MARILLA. *(Resolutely)* You'll go back to school
tomorrow, Anne. I'll see to that.

ANNE. *(Pleading)* Please, Marilla, try to compre-
hend the position I find myself in. I fear that I'm
not long for this world. *(Wistfully)* But if I should
die tomorrow, at least I've partaken of the joy of
having had a home and somebody to belong to. I've
been Anne of Green Gables, and that's better than
being any other Anne in the world. When I'm
buried, please place a lock of Diana's hair in my
casket, and I'm sure Matthew will want to put a
box of my favorite chocolates along with it. You
can inform everybody in Avonlea that I died of a
broken heart caused by an excess of grief.

MARILLA. *(Irately)* I don't think there's much
fear of your dying of grief as long as you can talk,
Anne. We'll discuss your going back to school later.

ANNE. *(Gratefully)* Thanks, Marilla. It's always
helpful to *infer* unpleasant things until later on. I'll
have to imagine so hard and for ever so long in
order to believe that my freckles aren't too disfigur-
ing.

MARILLA. I do wish you'd pay less attention to
your looks and more attention to holding your temper in check. Handsome is as handsome does.

ANNE. *(Gravely)* I've heard that said before but
I doubt it, Marilla. Next to being beautiful and
having a white dress with puffed sleeves I can't
imagine what could be more scrumptious. Scrump-

tious is a new word that I learned today for the first time. And I wrote the most beautiful essay at school today, and now I wish I hadn't turned it in.

MARILLA. What was the essay about?

ANNE. *(Enthusiastically)*   About   Benjamin Franklin's life. How he was born a poor boy and how he educated himself. And then one day when he was walking along the street in Philadelphia, he met the most beautiful girl he'd ever seen. She didn't even have one freckle, and he fell in love with her. He worked hard and several years later he met this same girl again and he proposed to her, and a short time later they got married and *he discovered electricity.* (MATTHEW *emits a series of loud chuckles.* MARILLA *glares at him angrily and he subsides abruptly.)*

MARILLA. *(Rising)* Anne, you never seem to remember anything I tell you to do. Who forgot to hang up their clothes before they went to sleep?

ANNE. *(Jumping up quickly and facing* MARILLA *proudly)* I know the answer to that, Marilla, but you didn't tell me. I learned it at Sunday School. It was Adam.

MARILLA. *(Tossing her head indignantly)* I declare I never met a girl like you. Now remember that Mrs. Allan is coming this afternoon for tea. I do hope that layer cake you baked turned out all right. *(Crosses up to arch and pauses, turning to face* ANNE*)* I've got to find my gold brooch with the amethysts—the one I've had so many years. It will hold my collar in place in the front. *(Exits* C. *to* L.*)*

ANNE. *(Crossing to* L. *of* MATTHEW *and placing a hand on his arm affectionately)* Dear Matthew, I'm so sorry I broke my promise to you today. If only my temper would give me some warning beforehand. But I don't suppose we are ever warned before we lose things or we'd manage somehow to keep them.

MATTHEW. *(Rising and reaching into his trouser pocket)* I bought you a little knife in town today, Anne, so's you could sharpen your pencils at school. Now that you ain't going back you won't have any use for it, I'm afraid. *(He brings forth a small knife from trouser pocket and hands it to* ANNE.*)*

ANNE. *(Examining the knife admiringly)* But of course I'll need this knife just the same. I'm going to continue my lessons right here at home and I'll always have pencils to sharpen. *(Sadly)* Oh, dear, what a shame that I spent all my money. *(Looks up at* MATTHEW *ruefully.)*

MATTHEW. *(Bewildered)* Huh?

ANNE. *(Frowning)* I ought to give you a piece of money in exchange for this knife or our friendship might be cut right in two. *(Crosses to sofa* L.C. *and sits, a thoughtful expression on her face.)*

MATTHEW. *(Crossing to* R. *of sofa and placing a hand in his trouser pocket)* I'll lend you some money, Anne. Will that be all right?

ANNE. *(Shaking her head "no")* It has to be my own money, Matthew. *(Looking up at him anxiously)* You'll try not to allow anything to mar our friendship until I can save a five-cent piece, won't you?

MATTHEW. *(Gravely)* I'll try not to let anything happen between us, Anne.

ANNE. *(Gayly)* Then I'll enjoy using my knife, and I'll imagine that it's a royal dagger. *(Gratefully)* Oh, Matthew, you don't know how happy you've made me with this gift. Next to a white dress with puffed sleeves, I'd rather have it than anything I can think of. *(Eagerly)* You don't suppose Marilla will object to my having a royal dagger, do you? I can't make Marilla out. There are times when I sort of think she'd like to melt a little, but she never does.

MATTHEW. *(Gravely)* We-el, I dunno. She's peculiar, Marilla is. (ANNE *pushes over* L. *on sofa and motions for him to join her. He sits* R. *of* ANNE.)

ANNE. *(Bewildered)* Peculiar? How?

MATTHEW. *(Slowly)* Well, I don't know as I'd better try to tell you and then again perhaps I better had. You see, Anne, Marilla's never had any children 'round her before. That makes a difference.

ANNE. *(Nodding assent; gravely)* I know. If Marilla had raised as many children as I have she'd understand them better.

MATTHEW. *(Bewildered)* Huh?

ANNE. I mean the Williams children and the little ones at the orphanage.

MATTHEW. Oh, yes—to be sure. You see, Anne, Marilla's not given to saying the things that are in her heart, but she feels them just the same. She's hard on the outside but soft on the inside, if you see what I mean.

ANNE. *(Understandingly)* I know. But I've often wondered why people are like that and I can't tell you any more than I know what thistles grow for. Ever so many years ago when I was just a teeny-weeny little girl, I heard a lady say, "Don't wait until I die to put roses on my grave. Give them to me while I'm living." Did you ever hear that, Matthew?

MATTHEW. *(Scratching the side of his head)* Well, I dunno. Can't say that I have and I can't say that I haven't. If I have I've plumb forgotten it.

ANNE. *(Gravely)* I never forget anything that's beautiful. When I saw that Gil—I mean, a certain boy for the first time today, I thought he was beautiful and that I'd never forget him, but now—now— *(Pauses abruptly.)*

DIANA. *(Off* R., *outside of door; excitedly)* Anne, Anne, where are you?

ANNE. *(Jumping up and clapping her hands together delightedly)* It's my Diana! *(Rushes over to* R. *door and opens same.* MATTHEW *rises and smiles at her admiringly, then crosses to door* L.1 *and exits.* DIANA BARRY, *a pretty girl about the same age as* ANNE, *enters through screen door* R. *She, too, may be played by an older girl who looks younger because of her small size.* DIANA *is inclined to be plump. She is of an affectionate nature, earnest and sincere, but lacks* ANNE'S *great imagination. She is dressed in a becoming summer frock with wide puffed sleeves. Her single braid of hair is tied with an elaborate bow of ribbon; no hat. As* DIANA *enters she rushes to* ANNE *and they embrace affectionately.)*

DIANA. *(To* ANNE, *after the embrace)* Oh, Anne, I was so afraid you'd keep your promise and harm yourself in some way.

ANNE. *(As she leads* DIANA *down to below sofa* L.C.; *gravely)* I was going to, Diana, but it just occurred to me that Gil—I mean, a certain boy would think I had done it because of him, and I wouldn't want him to have that satisfaction. *(They sit on sofa,* DIANA R. *of* ANNE.)

DIANA. *(Relieved)* Well, I'm certainly glad you've decided to be sensible about it. (ANNE *retains the knife* MATTHEW *has given her in her hand all during this scene.)* Oh, Anne, Mother is terribly upset.

ANNE. *(Anxiously)* What about?

DIANA. *(In troubled tones)* That Rachel Lynde woman was over to our house, and she told Mother her version of the affair at school today, and Mother said perhaps I'd better not come over here any more.

ANNE. *(Trembling with fear)* Not come over? Oh, Diana, does your mother realize what it would mean to me to have my bosom friend torn asunder? *(Rises)* My love for you in *inextinguishable.*

DIANA. *(Rising and facing her)* And so is mine for you, Anne.

ANNE. *(Eagerly)* Do you really mean that, Diana?

DIANA. *(Nodding vigorously)* Of course. Didn't you know?

ANNE. *(Shyly)* Why, I hoped you liked me, but I didn't know you loved me the way a real bosom friend should. *(Gravely)* You know, you're the first really bosom friend I ever had, and I could never care for anybody as I do for you.

DIANA. *(Pleading)* Then do, please, say that you'll forgive Gilbert Blythe and come back to school tomorrow.

ANNE. *(Shaking her head "no")* My feelings have been hurt *excrutiatingly,* Diana. You must never mention that boy's name in my presence again.

DIANA. Will Marilla let you stay home?

ANNE. *(Firmly)* She'll have to.

DIANA. *(Greatly upset)* Oh, Anne, I do think you're being mean. Mr. Phillips will make me sit with that dreadful Josie Pye—I know he will because she is sitting alone. *(Takes over to below table* R.C.*)* Do come back, Anne.

ANNE. *(Crossing to* C.*)* I'd do almost anything in the world for you, Diana—honestly I would. *(With great earnestness)* I'd let myself be torn limb from limb if it would do you any good. But I can't do this, so please don't ask. You harrow my very soul.

DIANA. *(Facing* ANNE*)* Just think of all the fun you'll miss. We are going to build the loveliest house down by the brook, and we're going to organize a girls' bowling team and have tournaments. Have you ever bowled, Anne?

ANNE. *(Distastefully)* No, and I don't ever intend to. I don't think it's at all ladylike to knock things down even if they are only *unanimate* objects. Bowling is all right for fat boys who work in laundries.

DIANA. *(Solemnly)* Oh, Anne, if you don't come to school and we don't see each other any more—

ANNE. *(Breaking in quickly)* I was thinking just last night that we'd have to be parted sooner or later anyhow, Diana. *(She takes over to just L. of Di-ANA)* I'm just a poor orphan and you'll grow up to be a rich lady and marry a Dook or a Lord or something. And then you'll have to leave me. And I've been imagining it all out—the wedding and everything.

DIANA. *(Astonished)* Why, Anne, I—

ANNE. *(Breaking in on her hastily)* You'll be dressed for your wedding in snowy satin with a veil and looking as regal as a queen; and me, the bridesmaid, in a white dress with puffed sleeves, but with a breaking heart hid beneath my smiling face. And then, bidding my Diana goodbye-e-e— *(Pauses and emits a loud sob.)*

DIANA. *(Placing an arm around her comfortingly)* But that won't happen for ever so many years.

ANNE. *(Stifling her sobs; pleadingly)* Oh, Diana, will you promise not to ever forget the friend of your youth no matter what dearer friends may make overtures to thee? *(DIANA opens her mouth as though to speak but ANNE continues without giving her a chance)* I read a book at the orphanage once and it was called "The Maidens' Farewell," and the two girls addressed each other as *thou* and *thee*. It was so romantic that I think we ought to try it. Wilt thee?

DIANA. *(Drawing her arm away and drawing herself up to her full height)* I wilt!

ANNE. *(Happily)* Diana, thy memory wilt shine like a star over my lonely life. And even though thou art a bride and go to live among strangers my heart wilt ever be faithful to thee.

DIANA. *(Melodramatically)* And mine to thee. *(Eagerly)* Oh, Anne, wilt thou walk half way home with me now?

ANNE. *(Nodding assent)* And shall we thou and thee each other on the way?

DIANA. *(Happily)* Yes, let's. I wilt if thou wilt. *(They laugh happily and rush up to door R., where they exit merrily. MATTHEW enters L.1, crosses to sofa and sits.)*

MARILLA. *(Outside L. of arch; loudly)* Matthew, is Anne down there?

MATTHEW. *(Looking around anxiously)* We-el, I dunno. Can't say that she is and I can't say that she ain't.

MARILLA. *(Enters C. from L.; angrily)* I do declare, Matthew, you'd try the patience of a saint. Don't you know whether Anne is here or not? *(Comes down to R. of sofa.)*

MATTHEW. Nope, I don't. But I do know she was here a few minutes ago, and so was Diana Barry.

MARILLA. *(Greatly displeased)* Then I suppose Anne has gone over to Diana's house with her. I do hope she doesn't stay too long.

MATTHEW. *(Looking at her out of the corner of his eye)* Well, I can't say that she will and I can't say that she won't. She might come right home, and then again she mightn't. *(Apologetically)* You know, Marilla, there are times when I think you are a little hard on Anne, if you don't mind my saying so.

MARILLA. *(Angrily)* Well, I most certainly do

mind, Matthew Cuthbert. So I'm hard on her, am I?

MATTHEW. *(Meekly)* Now don't get upset, Marilla. I'm your brother and the only one you have or ever will have.

MARILLA. *(Testily)* That's something to be thankful for. What made you say I was hard on Anne? Has she been complaining?

MATTHEW. *(Hastily)* You'd oughta know better than that, Marilla. You know Anne ain't the sort to complain. I was just thinking of the old saying when I remarked that.

MARILLA. *(Bewildered)* What old saying?

MATTHEW. *(Rising; impressively)* Don't you remember? It goes something like this: "Don't wait until I'm dead to put roses on my grave—put them on now!"

MARILLA. *(Astonished)* Put roses on your grave now? Matthew Cuthbert, have you lost what little mind you had? How can a body put roses on a grave before it's graved? Where did you ever get such nonsense from? Did Anne tell it to you?

MATTHEW. *(Resuming his seat on sofa; uncomfortably)* Well, I ain't saying that she did and I ain't saying that she didn't. I ain't saying but what she might have and I ain't saying but what she mightn't.

MARILLA. *(Severely)* That means that she did. I might have known it was some of her tom-foolery. I hope she hurries home. You remember my amethyst brooch, Matthew? *(He nods.)* I can't find it anywhere.

MATTHEW. Did you look in your bureau?

MARILLA. *(Impatiently)* I've hunted high and low for it. Ive taken out all the drawers of my bureau and looked in every crack and cranny.

MATTHEW. *(Casually)* This ain't the first time

you've misplaced it, Marilla. It's probably fallen behind your bureau.

MARILLA. *(Angrily)* I've already looked there, I tell you. I moved the bureau and everything else in my room. The brooch is not to be found.

MATTHEW. *(Calmly)* We-el, there's no sense in getting upset about it. You must keep cool.

MARILLA. *(Loudly and excitedly)* Cool? Would you be cool if you'd lost a valuable brooch?

MATTHEW. We-el, I can't say as to that. I never had a brooch to lose, so I can't say that I'd be cool or I can't say that I wouldn't.

MARILLA. *(Impatiently)* Oh, why did Anne have to go out just this afternoon when I'm expecting Mrs. Allan and there's so much to do?

ANNE. *(Outside of door R.; loudly and tearfully)* Matthew, oh, Matthew, I knew something terrible would happen.

MARILLA. *(Despairingly)* Land's sakes, if she ain't in trouble again! (MATTHEW *jumps up quickly and stands below sofa.* MARILLA *stands* R. *of sofa. They* BOTH *face the* R. *door as* ANNE *rushes in through door, sobbing loudly. She comes to* R. *of* MARILLA.)

MATTHEW. *(Anxiously)* What is it, Anne? What's the trouble?

ANNE. *(Tearfully)* I knew something dreadful would happen when you gave me that knife and I didn't have any money to give you in return. You see, Diana and I were going through The Haunted Wood—that's the name I've given to the wood just outside. We stopped to play and were having the grandest time calling each other *thee* and *thou* and—

MARILLA. *(Breaking in sternly)* Never mind that now, Anne. I've something important to ask you about. Have you see my amethyst brooch? I can't find it anywhere.

ANNE. *(Bewildered)* Yes, I saw it. Yesterday, while you were out at the Aid Society. I was passing your door when I saw the brooch on your cushion, so I just went in to look at it.

MARILLA. *(Demanding)* Did you touch it? Come, now, I want the truth.

ANNE. *(Hesitatingly)* Y-e-e-s, I took it up and pinned it on my breast just to see how it would look.

MARILLA. *(Wrathfully)* You had no business to do anything of the sort. I've told you that it's wrong to meddle. You shouldn't have gone into my room in the first place and you shouldn't have touched something that didn't belong to you in the second. Where did you put my pin?

ANNE. *(Looking directly at* MARILLA; *frankly)* Oh, I put it right back on the bureau. I hadn't it on a minute. Truly, I didn't mean to meddle. I didn't think about it being wrong to touch something that wasn't mine, but I see now that it was and I'll never do it again. That's one good thing about me. I never do the same naughty thing twice.

MARILLA. *(Sternly)* Anne, that brooch is gone. It's not upstairs. By your own confession you are the last one to have seen it. Now what have you done with it? Did you take it out and lose it?

ANNE. *(With great earnestness)* No, I didn't. I can't remember whether I put it back on the cushion or laid it in your china tray. But I'm perfectly certain I put it back.

MARILLA. *(Excitedly)* Well, the brooch is gone and nobody could have taken it but you.

ANNE. *(Tearfully)* Oh, dear, I'm positively sure I put it back, Marilla. I'm telling you the truth. I never took the pin out of your room and that's the honest truth, if I was to be led to the block for it—though I'm not very sure what a block is.

MARILLA. *(Resolutely)* I can see that you're telling me a falsehood, Anne, and I know that you took the brooch. There'll be no picnic for you tomorrow and I'll not allow you to see Mrs. Allan when she gets here. You're to go to your room and stay there until you confess.

ANNE. *(Dazed)* Not go to the picnic? Not see Mrs. Allan when I baked that delicious cake just for her? Oh, Marilla—

MARILLA. *(Breaking in sternly)* Go up to your room, and don't you dare leave it until you're ready to tell the absolute truth about that brooch. Mind me, now! (ANNE *lowers her head and walks slowly up to arch* C. *She turns and risks one pleading glance at* MARILLA, *who returns her glance with unflinching severity. Then* ANNE *emits a loud sob, lowers her head again and exits* C. *to* L. MATTHEW *sinks onto sofa.* MARILLA *crosses to chair* L. *of table* R.C. *and sits; angrily)* I don't know what I wouldn't sooner have had happen. Of course I don't suppose she meant to steal it or anything like that. She's just taken it along to play with and she's afraid to admit she lost it for fear of being punished. *(Darting an angry glance at* MATTHEW) Well, say something, can't you, Matthew?

MATTHEW. *(Uncomfortably)* What's the use? You've said all there is to say and more. (RACHEL *enters quickly through door* R., *followed by* MRS. BARRY. *The latter is without her hat and is nervous and upset.)*

RACHEL. *(As they enter)* Come right in, Missus Barry. Marilla won't mind. (RACHEL *comes down to* R. *of table* R.C. *and sits.)*

MRS. BARRY. *(Coming down to* L. *of* MARILLA; *apologetically)* I'm so sorry to have to burst in on you this way, my dear. But I'm terribly upset. I'm afraid I was wrong in my first estimate of Anne. She's absolutely vicious.

MARILLA. *(Rising)* What's that? (MATTHEW *rises quickly.)*

MRS. BARRY. *(Excited)* She wasn't content to scare Diana half to death with her imaginary tales of the wood outside the house being haunted and filled with ghosts and evil spirits, but after they left here this afternoon and were on their way to our house, Anne got Diana to pause while she cut off a lock of Diana's hair with a knife that she had.

MARILLA. *(Shrilly)* Why, the idea!

MRS. BARRY. And that isn't all. Anne told Diana that her penknife was a royal dagger, and then she insisted that they play a new game wherein Anne imagined she was Lucrecia Borgia. I don't suppose she meant to injure Diana, but she most certainly did stick the penknife into her. Diana has several scratches and marks on her throat.

MARILLA. *(Horrified)* Mercy days! Well, Matthew, what have you to say to that?

MATTHEW. *(Bewildered)* We-el, I dunno. I'd say it musta been kinda uncomfortable for Diana.

MRS. BARRY. *(To* MARILLA; *resolutely)* This is most regrettable, my dear, but in light of recent happenings I'm sure you'll understand how I feel when I say that I think it best to keep the two girls apart. I'll expect you to keep Anne away from my house. Good afternoon. *(Crosses up to door* R. *and exits hastily.)*

MARILLA. *(Sinking onto chair* L. *of table* R.C.*)* Well, I never! What next? (MATTHEW *crosses up extreme* L. *and fusses with the whatnot, his back to the audience.)*

RACHEL. *(Irately)* I'm glad that woman's gone. I never get a chance to get a word in edgewise when she's 'round. *(Facing* MARILLA; *triumphantly)* 'Course, Marilla, this is all your fault. You've brought the whole thing on yourself. If you had taken *my* advice, which you didn't, you'd never have allowed an orphan into your house.

ANNE. *(Enters* C. *from* L. *slowly and pauses in*

arch c.; *in a small, thin voice)* Please, Marilla, I'm ready to confess now.

MARILLA. *(Jumping up quickly)* Ah! I thought so. Come here this instant. (ANNE *comes down to* L. *of* MARILLA. MATTHEW *turns and listens intently.)* Let me hear what you have to say, then, Anne. (RACHEL *looks on wonderingly.)*

ANNE. *(Gravely)* I took the amethyst brooch, just as you said. When I pinned it on me it was so easy to imagine that I was Lady Cordelia Fitzgerald. I ran out of the house and started for The Lake Of Shining Water, and just as I got on top of the bridge that goes across the lake, I took the brooch off to admire it. That's when the awful thing happened.

MARILLA. *(Horrified)* You—you mean you lost my brooch?

ANNE. *(Hesitating)* We-el, not exactly. It just dropped out of my hand when I least expected it. It fell right into the water, and I just stood on the bridge and looked down with an expression of *hopeful despair*. I thought perhaps I could get the brooch back somehow, but it went down—down and sank forevermore beneath The Lake Of Shining Waters. And that's the best I can do at confessing, Marilla.

MARILLA. *(Wrathfully)* Anne, this is terrible! It was wicked of you to lose my brooch. I'm going to punish you severely for this. There'll be no picnic and you'll not see Mrs. Allan today.

ANNE. *(Tearfully)* Oh, but I've just *got* to see the heavenly expression on Mrs. Allan's face when she takes the first bite of that delicious layer cake I made expressly for her.

MARILLA. *(Sternly)* There's no sense in pleading, Anne. You'll not see Mrs. Allan and there will be no picnic for you.

ANNE. *(Sobbing)* But that's the reason I confessed. Oh, Marilla, please, please let me go to the picnic. Think of the ice-cream. For all you know I may never have a chance to taste ice-cream again.

RACHEL. *(Triumphantly)* I'm not at all surprised that she lost your brooch, Marilla. I've been expectin' somethin' like this to happen. *(Rising)* Lan's sakes, I almost forgot what I come over here for. I want to ask for the loan of your black shawl, Marilla, though I hate to bother you when you're so upset.

MARILLA. *(To RACHEL)* It's upstairs. I'll get it for you right now, Rachel. *(To ANNE; sternly)* You're not to leave this room until I get back, young lady. *(Crosses up and exits C. to L.)*

RACHEL. *(Resuming her seat; joyfully)* Mrs. Barry ain't goin' to let Diana speak to you no more, Anne. You've played together for the last time. *(MATTHEW comes down to L. of ANNE and regards her sympathetically.)*

ANNE. *(To RACHEL)* Not play with Diana? Did Mrs. Barry say so?

RACHEL. *(Severely)* She said a lot more'n that, if you'd care to know it. Now, if you ask *my* advice, you'll—

ANNE. *(Breaking in on her tearfully)* Oh, whatever am I to do? I'll simply have to see Diana. I just can't live if I don't. *(As though suddenly inspired)* I know. I'll go back to school tomorrow, and if that Gil—I mean, if a certain boy attempts to speak to me I'll just look right through him.

RACHEL. You won't be able to speak to Diana, though.

ANNE. *(Resignedly)* Well, even though we meet as strangers, at least I'll have the satisfaction of looking at her. And maybe some day Mrs. Barry will repent and Diana and I will be just as we always were. *(Loud KNOCK on door R.)*

MATTHEW. *(Starting for door R.)* Now who can that be, I wonder? (ANNE *takes over* L. *to below*

sofa L.C. MATTHEW *opens door and looks off* R.)
Oh, it's you, Moody. Come right in. (MATTHEW
retraces his steps to just R. *of sofa as* MOODY SPUR-
GEON, *a tall, awkward appearing boy of fifteen,
enters through door* R. *He is dressed in overalls and
heavy working shoes and wears a broad brimmed
straw hat, the sort country boys wear when they
work in the fields.* MOODY *has a permanent expression of sadness on his face and never has been
known to smile.*)

MOODY. *(Crossing to* C. *and coming down to* R.
of MATTHEW; *embarrassed)* I—I brung yer pig
back, Mister Matthew. She's in the barn.

MATTHEW. *(Bewildered)* Brought Dimples back?
But what'd you do that for, Moody?

MOODY. *(Nervously)* Why—er—you see, sir, we
want a healthy pig. My Paw's afraid this one ain't
long for this world.

MATTHEW. *(Astonished)* Why, that pig was in
perfect health this morning when I saw her last.

MOODY. *(Firmly)* Well, she ain't in perfect health
now. She's got funny colored blotches all over her.
We're a-skeered to butcher her for fear we'd all get
took sick.

ANNE. *(Tragically)* Oh Matthew, my troubles
are just piling up on me today. I'm responsible for
those ugly blotches on Dimples.

MATTHEW. *(Turning to her; bewildered)* Eh?

ANNE. *(Nodding assent)* Yes. You see, yesterday, while Marilla was out, a peddler came to the
back door, and he offered to sell me a box of freckle-remover for only ten cents. It was the last box
he had and he said it was guaranteed to remove
freckles from anybody.

MATTHEW. *(Bewildered)* We-el, what's that got
to do with the pig?

ANNE. *(Tragically)* I bought the freckle-remover
and I thought I'd try it out on Dimples because I

love her so much and I know she must suffer with all those freckles on her, same as I do from mine.

RACHEL. *(Rising hastily; astonished)* You mean you put freckle-remover on a pig, Anne Shirley?

ANNE. *(Tearfully)* Yes, and now poor Dimples is all broken out and my heart is broken. I just felt it go dead inside me. *(Places her hand over her heart)* Matthew, you'll have to punish me something dreadful for this.

MATTHEW. *(Smiling at her sympathetically)* We-el, I dunno. Reckon Marilla is able to do enough punishing for the entire family. *(Turning to MOODY)* Come along, Moody, and I'll give you another pig. I'll find one for you that ain't tainted with freckle-remover. *(Chuckles softly and starts for door R.)*

MOODY. *(To ANNE; dismally)* I'll be seein' you at the picnic tomorrer, Anne. I'll buy you a sody pop if my Paw gives me the money he owes me, which he prob'ly won't. 'Bye. *(Crosses up to door R. and exits.)*

RACHEL. *(Resuming her seat on chair)* Well, Anne Shirley, if you don't beat all. Puttin' freckle-remover on a pig.

ANNE. *(Wistfully)* I thought it would be so romantic to cure Dimples of her freckles before I got rid of my own.

MARILLA. *(Enters C. from L., carrying a black shawl. Her other hand is tightly closed as though she holds something inside of it. As she enters; excitedly)* Anne Shirley, what did you mean just now by storying to me? *(Coming down to R. of ANNE)* When I went to my trunk to get this shawl out, there was my brooch caught in one of the folds. *(Opens her hand and holds up the brooch)* I remembered then that I wore this shawl yesterday, and when I took it off I placed it on the bureau for a minute. I suppose my brooch got caught in it somehow. But I can't for the life of me understand why you went into that long rigmarole about losing it.

ANNE. *(Wearily)* Well, Marilla, when I told you the truth you wouldn't believe me, and I try so hard all the time to make you happy, so I just *imagined* I'd lost the brooch, thinking that would please you. And now may I please cut the layer cake, because Mrs. Allan will be here any minute.

MARILLA. *(Grudgingly)* Well, I'm afraid we were both wrong. It wasn't right for you to confess to a thing you hadn't done, but I drove you to it, so we'll just say no more about it. Cut the cake, and mind you do it carefully, and I'll think over what I said about the picnic tomorrow.

ANNE. *(Her entire manner changing to one of joy)* Oh, Marilla, you're so good to me! *(She rushes over to MARILLA, reaches up and throws her arms around her, kissing her on the cheek.)*

MARILLA. *(Pushing ANNE away from her; embarrassed)* I don't go in for kissing and that nonsense, Anne. It's sheer foolishness. Go and get the cake ready to serve. (ANNE *turns and exits* L.I. MARILLA *takes over to* L. *of table* R.C. *and hands* RACHEL *the shawl)* Here you are, Rachel. But for you I wouldn't have known that my pin was here instead of at the bottom of the lake where I thought it to be.

RACHEL. *(Rising and taking the shawl; stiffly)* You made a mistake just now by saying that Anne could go to the picnic tomorrow, Marilla. If you'd asked *my* advice, which you didn't, I'd have told Anne that she couldn't go.

MARILLA. *(Severely)* When I want your advice I'll ask for it, Rachel. Anne's my girl now and I reckon I can raise her without outside interference.

RACHEL. *(Tossing her head stiffly)* Well, you needn't bite my head off. Can't a body say a word

in this house without bein' taken to task for it? I
really believe you enjoyed havin' her kiss you just
now. *(Points a finger at* MARILLA *accusingly.)*

MARILLA. *(Horrified)* The idea! *(She rubs her
cheek distastefully where* ANNE *has kissed her, then
pins her brooch onto her waist)* You're just talking
rubbish and you know it. *(DOORBELL jangles off
up* R. MARILLA *registers great excitement)* Oh,
dear, here's Mrs. Allan now, and I forgot to put on
my new lace collar that Anne gave me. *(To* RA-
CHEL*)* Excuse me, Rachel. I'll have to answer the
bell. *(Crosses up and exits hastily* C. *to* R.*)*

RACHEL. *(Tossing her head indignantly)* Humph!
Marilla Cuthbert can't fool me! *(She crosses to door
R. and exits, taking the shawl with her.)*

MARILLA. *(Off up* R.; *cordially)* Of course we
expected you. Come right in, Mrs. Allan. *(Enters
C. from* R., *followed by* MRS. ALLAN, *a gracious and
charming woman in her early thirties. She has a
ready smile and a fine understanding of humanity.
Is becomingly garbed in a summer frock of modish
design, an attractive straw hat, gloves, purse, etc.*
MARILLA *comes down* R.C. MRS. ALLAN *is* L. *of her.)*

MRS. ALLAN. *(Eagerly)* Where is that Anne-
girl?

MARILLA. *(Motioning to sofa)* Do sit down and
make yourself comfortable, Mrs. Allan. (MRS.
ALLAN *sits on sofa and removes her gloves.)* Anne's
just cutting a layer cake that she baked especially
for you. She's taken a great fancy to you.

MRS. ALLAN. *(Greatly pleased)* She's a dear, and
so interesting. She makes me love her, and I like
people who make me love them. It saves me the
trouble of *making* myself love them. *(Laughs lightly.* MARILLA *sits* L. *of table* R.C. ANNE *enters* L.1,
*carrying a large tray that contains three glasses of
lemonade, three small plates with a piece of layer
cake on each plate, three forks and three napkins.)*

ANNE. *(As she sees* MRS. ALLAN; *enthusiastically)* Oh, Mrs. Allan, you look scrumptious. Just like the heroine of a novel. *(Crosses to* R.C., *below table, and places the tray on table.)*

MRS. ALLAN. *(Smiling at* ANNE*)* Thank you, my dear.

ANNE. *(Picking up a plate containing a large piece of layer cake, a napkin and a fork and rushing over to* R. *of sofa; eagerly)* I can hardly wait to have you sample my layer cake. Marilla taught me how to bake it. I've followed her directions *unplicitly.*

MRS. ALLAN. *(Restraining a desire to laugh; graciously)* Umm, the cake looks splendid. I know I'm going to enjoy this. *(She takes the plate of cake, the napkin and the fork from* ANNE.*)*

(WARN Curtain.)

MARILLA. *(Picking up a glass of lemonade from the tray and offering it to* ANNE*)* Give Mrs. Allan her lemonade, Anne. (ANNE *darts over to* L. *of* MARILLA, *takes the glass from her and crosses to* R. *of sofa.)*

MRS. ALLAN. *(Attacking the cake with her fork)* The lemonade can wait, Anne. I want to get the taste of this cake first. (MARILLA *sits* L. *of table* R.C. *complacently.* ANNE *stands* R. *of sofa, an eager expression on her face as* MRS. ALLAN *places a large bite of cake into her mouth.)*

ANNE. *(Her face wreathed in smiles)* Is it good, Mrs. Allan? As good as it looks?

MRS. ALAN. *(Making a wry face as she gets the real flavor of the cake)* Why—er—I believe there's something wrong with it, Anne. *(Rises quickly.)*

MARILLA. *(Jumping up apprehensively)* Anne Shirley, what did you put in that layer cake?

ANNE. *(Trembling with fear as she faces* MARILLA*)* Why, nothing, Marilla. Nothing except some vanilla extract—

MARILLA. *(Shrilly)* Where did you get the vanilla extract from?

ANNE. *(Fearfully)* From the kitchen pantry on the bottom shelf.

MARILLA. *(Shrilly)* I might have known you'd do it. I forgot to tell you that I emptied the vanilla extract that was in that bottle into a cup and put something else in the bottle instead.

ANNE. *(Aghast)* Oh, Marilla, how awful! What was it you put in the bottle?

MARILLA. *(Loudly and shrilly)* The entire cake will have to be thrown out or whoever eats it will be poisoned.

ANNE and MRS. ALLAN. *(Together; fearfully)* Poisoned?

MARILLA. *(Excitedly)* Anne, you've gone and flavored that cake with *Chloroform Liniment!* (MRS. ALLAN *emits a loud and startled shriek and sinks onto the sofa, frightened.* MARILLA *glares at* ANNE *angrily.* ANNE *bursts into tears as the Curtain falls swiftly.)*

END OF ACT TWO

ACT THREE

Scene I

Scene: *Same as previous Act.*

Time: *Two years later; an afternoon in April.*

Discovered at Rise: Matthew *sits* l. *of table,* r. *of* c., *reading a newspaper. He is dressed in his best blue suit, stiff white collar and black string bow tie. His shoulders are bent more than in the earlier portions of the play and he has aged perceptibly. As soon as the Curtain rises,* Anne *enters* l.2. *She wears a neat print or gingham dress with tight sleeves and severely plain, but the skirt has been lengthened to denote her added two years. Her hair, too, is dressed high on her head in modern fashion. White shoes and stockings complete her outfit. She carries a pencil and a pad of white foolscap paper in her hand.*

Anne. *(As she enters and sees* Matthew; *joyously)* Matthew! I didn't know you'd gotten back from town. Where's Marilla? *(Crosses to* l. *of* Matthew.)

Matthew. *(Smiling at* Anne) I just got back a few minutes ago. Marilla stayed in town for awhile.

Anne. *(Eagerly)* Is she going to do some shopping?

Matthew. *(Evasively)* We-el, I dunno. Can't say

that she is and I can't say that she ain't. Don't know
if she will and don't know that she won't.

ANNE. *(Perplexed)* But how is she going to get
back to Green Gables?

MATTHEW. Mrs. Allan is with her. She's going to
drive Marilla back here.

ANNE. *(Thoughtfully)* I can't realize that it's two
whole years since I almost poisoned dear Mrs. Allan
with the cake I baked for her. She was so sweet and
forgiving. She went out of her way to prove that
she is a kindred spirit.

MATTHEW. *(Smiling broadly)* 'Pears like that list
is growing mighty rapid, Anne.

ANNE. *(Gravely)* Well, now, let me see. Of
course, you head the list—that goes without saying.
Next comes my dear Diana, my bosom friend. Then
Mrs. Allan—I've always loved her. I can't make up
my mind about Mrs. Barry, although she has been
simply elegant to me since I saved her youngest
daughter's life the time she was out and Diana came
running over here with little Minnie May. She actually begged me to play with Diana again, so I suppose she ought to be added to the list. Marilla is still
doubtful—I've never tried to kiss her since that time
she said I could go to the picnic. *(Firmly)* But there
are two people whom I know will never be kindred
spirits.

MATTHEW. *(Curiously)* Two?

ANNE. *(Nodding vigorously)* One of them is Gil
—I mean, a certain boy whose name I never mention and the other is that Josie Pye. I've tried so
hard to like her but I don't feel that I've made any
actual progress. I suppose if there's such a thing as
half way kindred spirits Mrs. Rachel might be on
that list. She's nicer to me than she used to be.
(Crosses to chair behind table R.C. *and sits, emitting
a deep sigh)* Oh, dear, I can't believe that tomorrow

is my birthday. I'm afraid that the trouble with most of us is that we live too long. *(Sighs again.)*

MATTHEW. *(Anxiously)* Mrs. Lynde ain't been over today so far, has she, Anne?

ANNE. *(Shaking her head "no")* Matthew, you're trying to conceal something from me. I know it. You keep asking about Mrs. Rachel and you've never been interested in her before.

MATTHEW. *(Nervously)* Why—er—I— Now, Anne—

ANNE. *(Breaking in quickly)* Matthew, I do hope you aren't planning to let the Lyndes have the ten acres of land that adjourns our farm. I wouldn't have you sell it for anything. It's too beautiful to part with and I'd miss it terribly. *(Sighing forlornly)* Oh, dear, I do feel so sad today.

MATTHEW. *(Greatly concerned)* Sad? What about?

ANNE. *(Solemnly)* Well, I was thinking awhile ago that the time will come when this fine house will be nothing but crumbling stone and you and Marilla and I will be nothing but dust and ashes and scattered all over it.

MATTHEW. *(Gravely)* I wouldn't worry none about that if I was you, Anne.

ANNE. *(Gratefully)* Wouldn't you? Oh, it's such a relief to hear you say that, Matthew. You're always so comforting and try your best to *reinsure* me. So many people laugh at the things I say, although I never can understand why they do. I never intend to be funny. *(Greatly upset)* Oh, dear, I forgot to add Miss Stacy's name to the list of kindred spirits. I just love her and ever since she took Mr. Phillip's place at school I've had so much more scope for my imagination. *(Starts to write on her foolscap pad.)*

MATTHEW. *(Resuming the reading of his paper)* Are you working on my accounts now, Anne?

ANNE. *(Continuing to write)* Oh, no, I've finished

them. This is a story I'm writing for our story club. We have to make up all our stories out of our own heads. It's very conducive, Matthew.

DIANA. *(Outside of door* R., *loudly)* Anne—yoo hoo— Oh, Anne, where are you?

ANNE. *(Jumping up breathlessly)* There's Diana now. *(Rushes over to* R. *door and opens same)* Come on in, Diana. (MATTHEW *rises, smiles, crosses to door* L.I *and exits, taking his paper with him.* DIANA *enters* R. *She wears a light-colored frock with wide puffed sleeves. Her skirt has been lengthened, too, and her hair has been "put up." The two girls greet each other affectionately, then come down* C., ANNE R. *of* DIANA.)

DIANA. *(Eagerly)* What were you doing just now, Anne?

ANNE. *(Rushing over to table* R.C. *and picking up her foolscap pad)* I'm just finishing my latest story. I do hope Miss Stacy will like it.

DIANA. *(Bewildered)* Finishing it? Why, I haven't even started mine. I never know what to write about. *(Crosses to sofa* L.C. *and sits.)*

ANNE. *(Crossing to* R. *of sofa; enthusiastically)* Why, it's as easy as wink.

DIANA. *(Complainingly)* It's easy for you because you have an imagination. What would you do if you'd been born without one? What's the name of your story?

ANNE. *(The foolscap pad in her hand)* It's called "The Jealous Rival; or, In Death Divided." I read it to Marilla, that is, all she would listen to, and she said it was stuff and nonsense.

DIANA. *(Agog with curiosity)* What's the story about?

ANNE. *(With extreme seriousness)* It's very sad, Diana. I cried like a child when I wrote it. It's all about two beautiful maidens called Cordelia Montmorency and Geraldine Seymo   who   in the same village and were devotedly attached to each other. Cordelia was a regal brunette with a coronet of midnight hair and dusky flashing eyes. Geraldine was a queenly blond with hair like spun gold and *velvety purple* eyes.

DIANA. *(Dubiously)* I never saw anybody with purple eyes.

ANNE. *(Facing* DIANA*)* Neither did I. I just imagined them. I wanted something that wasn't common, something *instinctive.* Geraldine had an alabaster brow, too. I've found out what an alabaster brow is. That's one reason I don't mind having birthdays once every year. You know so much more on each *preceding* birthday.

DIANA. Don't you mean succeeding, Anne?

ANNE. *(Happily)* There, you see, now you're starting to use your imagination.

DIANA. *(Doubtfully)* Well, what became of Geraldine and Cordelia?

ANNE. *(Glancing at her foolscap pad)* They grew in beauty side by side until they were sixteen. Then Bertram DeVere came to their native village and fell in love with the fair Geraldine. Bertram proposed to her and that took up a whole page. I made it very romantic. I rewrote that speech five times and I look upon it as my masterpiece. So they became engaged, but then, alas, shadows began to darken over their path.

DIANA. *(Eagerly)* What sort of shadows?

ANNE. *(Dramatically)* Cordelia was secretly in love with Bertram herself and when she heard they were engaged she vowed that Geraldine should never wed him. But she pretended to be Geraldine's friend just the same though all her love had turned to hate.

DIANA. *(Tremendously impressed)* How awful! What happened?

ANNE. *(Impressively)* One evening they were standing on the bridge over a turbulent stream and

Cordelia, thinking they were alone, pushed Geraldine over the brink with a wild, mocking, "Ha! Ha! Ha!" But Bertram saw it all and he plunged immediately into the current, shouting, "Fear not, I shall save thee, my peerless Geraldine!"

DIANA. *(Jumping up, excitedly)* And did he?

ANNE. *(Sorrowfully)* Alas, no! He had forgotten to bring his water wings and he couldn't swim so they were both drowned, clasped in each other's arms.

DIANA. *(Tearfully)* Oh, I don't like that. It's too sad.

ANNE. *(Enthusiastically)* But it's ever so much more romantic this way, Diana. It's better to wind up a story with a funeral than with a wedding. As for Cordelia, I'm just finishing up on her now. She went insane with remorse and was shut up in a lunatic asylum. I think that will be a poetical retribution for her crime.

DIANA. *(Sighing deeply)* How perfectly lovely. Oh, I do wish I had your imagination, Anne.

ANNE. *(Gravely)* It gets me into a lot of trouble at times. And upon certain occasions it makes me as blue as can be. When I think of the examinations at the end of the coming term, and how disappointed Matthew and Marilla will be if I fail—

DIANA. *(Breaking in loyally)* But you can't fail. Everybody in school says that you'll head the class unless Gil—

ANNE. *(Interrupting her angrily)* Diana, you ought to know better than to mention his name to me. If Gil—I mean, a certain boy, thinks he can annoy me by trying to get ahead of me in class, he's just got another think coming. *(She tosses her head disdainfully.)*

JOSIE. *(Off R., loud and excited)* Diana! Anne! Where are you?

ANNE. *(Distastefully)* It's that Josie Pye. I wonder what's happened now?

DIANA. *(Fretfully)* I do wish she'd move away from here. She saw me come in just now. *(Stands below sofa L.C. ANNE is R. of sofa. JOSIE rushes in R. She looks a great deal older than in previous Act. Her hair is piled up on top of her head and her skirt has been lengthened considerably. Wears a Summer frock of a garish design for comedy effect.)*

JOSIE. *(As she enters, excitedly)* Who d'you suppose I just saw? *(Rushes to R. of ANNE.)*

ANNE. *(Frigidly)* Good afternoon, Josie. Won't you sit down?

JOSIE. *(Shaking her head "no")* I can't stay but a minute. But I just had to tell you the news. Gilbert Blythe and Moody Spurgeon were havin' a fight over you, Anne.

ANNE. *(Placing her fingers to her ears)* I've warned you repeatedly not to mention Gil—er, that boy's name to me, Josie Pye.

DIANA. *(Loftily)* Everybody knows that we're not interested in Mr. Blythe's doings.

JOSIE. *(Spitefully)* You'd be int'rested in hearin' 'bout this, all right, 'cause somebody is likely to get hurt. *(Giggles.)*

DIANA. *(Agog with curiosity)* You mean that the boys were actually fighting over Anne?

ANNE. *(Removes her fingers from her ears. Sternly)* I don't suppose you'll be satisfied until you relate your gossip, so I'll try to bear up and listen to it. You may proceed, Josie.

JOSIE. *(Angrily)* Oh, I may, may I? Just for that I won't tell you at all. Seems to me that you're puttin' on a lotta airs for somebody who's just a orphan.

DIANA. *(Springing to ANNE's defense, she rushes over to L. of JOSIE and faces her angrily)* Don't you dare speak that way to Anne. (ANNE *lowers her head and takes over to below sofa, L.C.)* You ought to be ashamed of yourself, Josie Pye. (MARILLA *enters* c. *from* R. *and stands in arch* c., *unobserved by the* OTHERS. *She is attired in her best taffeta dress and wears the white lace collar* ANNE *gave her in previous Act around her neck, held in place by her gold brooch. A plain black straw sailor hat rests on her head. She has aged visibly, her hair being greyer than heretofore and her shoulders are slightly stooped.*)

JOSIE. *(Wrathfully)* What concern is it o' your'n, Diana Barry? You'd oughta change your name to Miss Busybody.

DIANA. *(Irately)* Yes, and you ought to change yours to—to—I think "Quince" Pye would fit you better than Josie.

ANNE. *(Gravely)* I can think of a name for her that would be even more conducive, Diana.

JOSIE. *(Darting an angry glance at* ANNE*)* Oh, is that so?

ANNE. *(Nodding assent)* It's the kind of pie I've always liked least of any.

DIANA. *(To* ANNE; *eagerly)* What is it, Anne?

ANNE. *(Hurling the word at* JOSIE*)* Raspberry! (JOSIE *emits an angry shout and starts toward* ANNE. DIANA *blocks her way.*)

MARILLA. *(Loudly and excitedly)* Here, here, what's going on here? (JOSIE *pauses. The three* GIRLS *turn and face* MARILLA.*)

JOSIE. I'm never goin' to speak to either o' you again. (JOSIE *turns and exits* R. *hastily, banging the door after her.* DIANA *stands behind table* R.C. ANNE *just below sofa* L.C.*)

MARILLA. *(Coming down* c., *sternly)* Well, Anne, what have you been up to now? I declare I don't dare leave this house or before my back is turned you are into some fresh mischief.

DIANA. *(Before* ANNE *has a chance to speak; spiritedly)* It wasn't Anne's fault this time, Miss

Marilla. That girl said terrible things to Anne, just because Anne asked her not to mention Gilbert Blythe's name to her. *(Suddenly realizing that she has used his name in* ANNE'S *presence and turning to* ANNE *contritely)* Oh, Anne, I'm so sorry I used his name. It just slipped out.

ANNE. *(Gravely)* I forgive you freely, dear Diana. I know that you didn't intend to wound me and that your motive was pure. *(Going to* L. *of* MARILLA.*)* Really, Marilla, I don't think you were justified in saying what you did just now. After all, I have shown remarkable improvement.

MARILLA. *(Removing her hat; severely)* Hmm! You have, have you?

ANNE. *(Nodding vigorously)* Oh, I know I'm a great trial to you, because I make so many mistakes. But then, just think of all the mistakes I don't make, although I might.

MARILLA. *(Crossing to table* L.C. *and placing her hat on same)* Humph!

ANNE. *(Contritely)* Sometimes when I'm with certain people I feel like a different Anne than when I'm with those I love. There seem to be such a lot of different Annes inside me and I never can make up my mind which one to be for any long period of time.

MARILLA. *(Turning to her severely)* Well, I wish you'd try to be the Anne who doesn't make any mistakes just for one day. *(She sits* L. *of table* L.C.*)*

ANNE. *(Facing her, solemnly)* I should think you'd be very hopeful about me, Marilla, because, you see, I never make the same mistake twice.

MARILLA. That don't make it any easier to bear while you're making them.

ANNE. *(Persistently)* Oh, but it ought to, really it should. You see, I'm comforted by the fact that I never do the same wrong thing twice. Now, it stands to reason that after I've gone through the entire list of mistakes there won't be any more for me to make and I won't be a trial to you any longer. *(Assumes a triumphant manner.)*

DIANA. *(As though suddenly remembering)* Anne, don't forget that this is the day we're to go rowing in Father's flat-bottomed boat.

ANNE. *(Enthusiastically)* Oh, Diana, as if I could ever forget that. I've been looking forward to it for days.

MARILLA. *(Sternly)* Now see that you two girls are careful, do you hear?

DIANA. *(Nodding assent)* Of course. I'll be waiting for you down by the pond, Anne. *(Rushes out R. MATTHEW enters L.I without his newspaper.)*

MARILLA. *(To MATTHEW)* It's a pity you couldn't take better care of Anne when I'm away, Matthew Cuthbert.

MATTHEW. *(Crossing to L. of sofa, bewildered)* I don't see anything wrong with Anne, Marilla. *(ANNE crosses up to arch C. and stands looking off R.)*

MARILLA. *(Rising and crossing to just below sofa)* You wouldn't see anything wrong with Anne no matter what she did.

RACHEL. *(Enters R. carrying a large dress box that is not wrapped in paper but is just tied with a piece of string. She wears a gingham house dress and her hair is considerably greyer than in previous Act.)* Matthew, I wanted to come over while Marilla was out but I just couldn't get here. *(Crosses to R. of table R.C.)*

MARILLA. *(Angrily)* What's that? Why shouldn't you come over while I'm here? *(Turning to MATTHEW)* Matthew Cuthbert, are you keeping a secret from your sister?

MATTHEW. *(Crossing to C.; uncomfortably)* Well, I ain't saying that I am and I ain't saying that I ain't. *(ANNE comes down to behind table R.C.)*

RACHEL. *(Garrulously)* Shucks, Marilla'll have to know 'bout it sooner or later. Tomorrow's Anne's birthday.

MARILLA. *(Crossing to L. of* MATTHEW, *agog with curiosity)* Rachel Lynde, what's that fool brother of mine done now? What's been going on behind my back?

MATTHEW. *(Taking a deep breath and summoning all his courage)* I'll tell you, Marilla. I've had a birthday present made for Anne.

ANNE. *(Delighted)* Oh, Matthew, have you really?

MARILLA. *(Astonished)* Without asking me about it?

MATTHEW. *(Nodding assent)* That's right. Open the box, Rachel. Might as well let Anne see it now. (RACHEL *removes the cord from the box and presents the box to* ANNE, *who places it on the table in front of her.)*

ANNE. *(Excitedly)* Oh, dear, I'm so excited I can hardly wait to get it open. (MATTHEW *crosses down to below sofa* L.C. ANNE *removes the cover of the box far enough so that she can see inside the box, then opens her mouth wide with astonishment)* Why —it's—it's—oh, no, it can't be!

RACHEL. *(Triumphantly)* It's a white dress with puffed sleeves that are wide enough even for you, Anne. I took your measurement from an old dress.

ANNE. *(Looking up, breathlessly)* Oh, this is an *epoch* in my life! *(Rushes over to* R. *of* MATTHEW *and throws her arms around him gratefully)* Oh, Matthew, you're the dearest, sweetest friend any girl ever had. I don't know how to thank you enough. Do you realize what this means to me? (MARILLA *crosses to behind table* R.C. *and inspects the dress without removing it from the box.)*

MATTHEW. *(To* ANNE; *embarrassedly)* Well, I can't say that I do and I can't say that I don't. (ANNE *continues to hug* MATTHEW *enthusiastically.)*

RACHEL. *(Proudly)* It's the very latest style. It's made somethin' beautiful, don't you think, Marilla?

ANNE. *(Stands* R. *of* MATTHEW, *holding onto his arm, and speaks before* MARILLA *has a chance to reply)* I can't tell you how I feel inside. It makes me realize that I ought to be a very model girl, indeed, and I always resolve that I will be in future. However, I'm going to make a very special effort this time. Oh, to think that that truly magnificent white dress with puffed sleeves belongs to me, Anne Shirley.

MARILLA. *(Severely)* Well, I must say that I think Anne has enough dresses. I've made her several *serviceable* ones, and anything else is sheer extravagance. There's enough material in these sleeves to make several blouses. Them sleeves are so big I don't see how she'll get through a door without going sideways.

RACHEL. *(Proudly)* I took more time with that dress than any I ever made.

MARILLA. *(Grudgingly)* Oh, it's real pretty, I'll admit. *(Jealously)* I don't suppose Anne will like what I got for her nearly as well, though I thought it was pretty at the time.

ANNE. *(Rushing over to* L. *of* MARILLA*)* Oh, you angel of a Marilla. How wonderful of you all to remember my birthday! *(Reverently)* We learned in Sunday School last week that the Lord always takes care of His own. I know it's true now because you and Matthew are as dear to me as if you were my very own parents.

MARILLA. *(In a vain effort to cover up her embarrassment)* Well, I—I— *(Directly to* MATTHEW*)* Matthew Cuthbert, what are you standing there staring into space for? Have you fed all the livestock in the barn?

MATTHEW. *(Grinning broadly)* We-el, I dunno,

but if I ain't nobody else will, that's certain. *(Sits on sofa, folds his arms, a sly grin on his face.)*

ANNE. *(Rapturously)* Oh, I simply must see Diana at once and acquaint her with my good fortune. Shall I hang the dress up, Marilla?

MARILLA. *(Picking up her hat from table* R.C.; *sternly)* You run along. I'll take care of hanging it up. Like as not you'll tear it the first time you put it on.

ANNE. Oh, no, I won't wear it often. I'll just spend most of my time gazing at it with sheer joy. I want Matthew to be the very first person to see me wear it because now I'll feel more like really being Anne of Green Gables than I've ever felt before. *(Rushes over to door* R., *then turns and faces* MATTHEW*)* I have the most comfortable feeling that the very first time I'm seen in that dress somebody is going to call me Lady Cordelia Fitzgerald. *(Laughs gayly, blows a kiss to* MATTHEW *and rushes out* R. RACHEL *sinks onto chair* R. *of table* R.C.*)*

MARILLA. *(Exasperated)* Well, I declare! Did you ever see the beat? I wonder where she gets enough breath to rattle on that way?

MATTHEW. *(Proudly)* Well, that dress means more to Anne than anything else could. You just don't understand her, Marilla.

MARILLA. *(Crossing to* L. *of sofa; defiantly)* Oh, so I don't understand Anne, eh? Well, let me tell you something, Matthew Cuthbert. I understand her well enough to have ordered the material for *three* dresses for Anne and I'm going to make them all myself with the *widest* puffed sleeves that anybody ever saw. *(Rushes over to table* R.C., *picks up the box with the dress in it, and sweeps up stage where she exits* C. *to* L.*)*

MATTHEW. *(Chuckling softly)* I sure got a rise outa Marilla that time.

RACHEL. *(Grinning broadly)* She was jealous

'cause you got the dress for Anne before she thought o' doin' it.

MATTHEW. But she'd never admit it. Marilla's got to break down some day and Anne is the only person who'll make her do it.

RACHEL. Well, mebbe you're right, but I doubt it. If I ever live to see the day that Marilla Cuthbert thaws out, then I'll believe in anythin'.

MATTHEW. *(As though suddenly remembering)* Your Tom said as how he'd be over to see me about that land proposition today, Rachel.

RACHEL. *(Rising and crossing to c.)* I'm here to talk 'bout it, Matthew. Reckon I can drive a business bargain same as my man.

MATTHEW. *(Rising; slyly)* Yes, I reckon you can drive anything.

RACHEL. *(Indignantly)* What?

MATTHEW. *(Apologetically)* I mean, I dunno. I ain't saying that you can and I ain't saying that you can't.

RACHEL. *(Resolutely)* We'll take the ten acres—got the cash to do it, too. But we've decided, Tom an' me, that your price is too high. I'll give you just one hundred dollars less than you're askin'. How about it?

MATTHEW. *(Fingering his chin thoughtfully)* We-el, I dunno. I might decide to take it and then again I mightn't. Can't say that I will and I can't say that I won't.

RACHEL. *(Irately)* You'll hafta make up your mind right now 'cause we got our eyes on Jed Todd's place. That has a house on it too and your land hasn't.

MATTHEW. *(Hesitatingly)* We-el, I reckon I'll let you have the ten acres at your own price, though it's mighty little for that much land.

RACHEL. *(Triumphantly)* Then it's a deal? *(He nods.)* We'll have the papers drawed up first thing tomorrow and I'll have the money on hand for you.

MATTHEW. *(Looking around the room anxiously to be sure they are alone, then back to* RACHEL*)* You've gotta promise me you won't say anything to Anne about this, Rachel. She's dead set against my parting with them ten acres.

RACHEL. I'll never tell her a word, Matthew. *(Taking a step* L. *near to him, agog with curiosity)* What are you goin' to do with this money?

MATTHEW. Why, you see, I want to send Anne away to school next year where she can get a real education. And it's going to take considerable money to do that.

RACHEL. Marilla's right. There's nothin' you wouldn't do for Anne.

MATTHEW. *(Weakly)* We-el, I dunno. You see, she's such a interesting little thing.

RACHEL. Now, if you'd asked my advice, which you didn't— *(DOORBELL jangles.* RACHEL *wheels about quickly and starts for door* R.*)* Lan's sakes, I gotta get home. We'll settle everythin' in the mornin', Matthew. *(Exits hastily.* MATTHEW *exits* C. *to* R. *There is a very short pause, then* MATTHEW *re-enters, followed by* GILBERT, *who wears a dark business suit, is well groomed and attractive as ever.)*

MATTHEW. *(As they enter)* Come right in, my boy. We haven't seen you for some time. *(Comes down to* R. *of sofa.)*

GILBERT. *(Crossing down to* R. *of* MATTHEW; *eagerly)* Is Anne at home, sir?

MATTHEW. Not right now. She left a little while ago.

GILBERT. *(Irately)* Honest, Mr. Cuthbert, I've never tried so hard to be friends with anybody in all my life as I have with Anne. But she's such a hot-headed kid she just continues to ignore me.

MATTHEW. We-el, I dunno. Anne's got a will of

her own. Reckon the best thing you can do is to forget her.

GILBERT. *(Desperately)* That's just it; I can't
seem to do it. I succeeded in getting Anne out of
my mind but I can't get her out of my heart.

(WARN Curtain.)

MATTHEW. *(Sympathetically)* Well, cheer up,
Son. Anne'll probably up and ask you to speak to
her some day.

GILBERT. *(Eagerly)* What makes you think that?

MATTHEW. We-el, I dunno. Reckon it's because
she keeps on saying she'll never speak to you and
girls always do just what they say they won't.

GILBERT. *(Wearily)* Not Anne. The School Board
have decided that Anne and I are to oppose each
other in a debate and I tried to get out of doing it
because I knew it would make her dislike me more
than ever. When that poor fish, Moody Spurgeon,
heard I was trying to beg off he said it was because
I was afraid Anne would put it all over me, so I
just had to go to the mat with him. I don't think
he'll have anything more to say about either Anne
or me.

JOSIE. *(Outside of door R., loudly and excitedly)*
Mister Cuthbert! Oh, Mr. Cuthbert! *(Rushes in R.
and comes down to R. of GILBERT)* Oh, the most
terrible thing has happened!

GILBERT. *(Anxiously)* What is it now, Josie?

JOSIE. *(Excitedly)* Anne an' Diana were out row-
in' an' they started to play "Lancelot an' Elaine" an'
Anne got up an' started actin' out a scene an' she fell
outa the boat an' into the water.

GILBERT *and* MATTHEW. *(Together, astonished)*
What?

JOSIE. *(As though exploding a bomb)* Anne can't
swim a stroke an' Diana's 'most frantic. There ain't
a sign o' Anne nowhere an' Diana's sobbin' that
Anne's drownded.

GILBERT. *(Tearing off his jacket, commanding)* Take me to the spot where Anne fell in, Josie. Hurry! *(Throws his jacket to the floor, grasps Jo-sie's arm and leads her to* R. *door, where they exit hastily.)*

MATTHEW. *(Dazedly)* Drowned! Oh, my poor little Anne. *(He comes to with a start, rushes over to door* R. *and exits quickly as the Curtain falls to denote a lapse of time.)*

END OF SCENE ONE

SCENE II

SCENE: *The same as previous Scene.*

TIME: *Two months later; an evening in June.*
    GILBERT'S *coat has been removed from the floor. A lighted oil lamp has been placed on table* R.C. *All LIGHTS on stage full up. LIGHTS outside of door* R. *to denote bright moonlight.*

DISCOVERED AT RISE: MARILLA *stands at door* R., *looking off* R. MATTHEW *enters* C. *from* R., *followed by* MRS. ALLAN. MARILLA *and* MATTHEW *are attired as in previous Scene and are without hats.* MRS. ALLAN *wears a becoming Summer frock and a hat to match and presents an attractive appearance.*

MRS. ALLAN. *(As she follows* MATTHEW *on; graciously)* I just dropped in for a minute to remind that Anne-girl that she's having a tea with us tomorrow. *(*MATTHEW *comes down to below sofa.* MRS. ALLAN *stands below arch* C. *and smiles at* MARILLA, *who turns and faces her.)* Good evening, Marilla. How nice you look!

MARILLA. *(Taking over to R. of table R.C.)* Anne's gadding 'round some place with Diana. We ain't seen much of her these past few days. Won't you sit, Mrs. Allan?

MRS. ALLAN. *(Coming down to chair L. of table R.C. and sitting)* Thanks. My, but weren't you proud of Anne this afternoon? I was. Just think, she headed her class and passed with the highest honors of any girl in Avonlea. (MATTHEW *sits on sofa.*)

MARILLA. *(Severely)* I'd be prouder still if she didn't talk so much, though I must admit I'm kinda getting used to it.

MATTHEW. *(Dryly)* Which is Marilla's way of admitting that she was mighty proud of Anne.

MRS. ALLAN. *(Restraining a desire to laugh)* Mr. Allan and I are both very happy about Anne. She's the most remarkable girl we've ever met. *(Eagerly)* Has she spoken to Gilbert Blythe yet?

MATTHEW. Not yet. She won't even mention his name.

MARILLA. *(Stiffly)* Anne's mighty stubborn. She takes after Matthew in that. (MATTHEW *emits a loud "Ha!"*)

MRS. ALLAN. *(Ruefully)* Poor Gilbert! I was hoping that after he saved her life and rescued Anne she would at least thank him.

MARILLA. I think she wanted to but she's so proud she hates to give in. I never could understand that in folks, could you, Matthew?

MATTHEW. *(Looking directly at her; pointedly)* We-el, I dunno. Can't say that I do and I can't say that I don't, but I *do say* that I'd oughta understand it after living with *you* all these years.

MARILLA. *(Jumping up; irately)* Well, the idea!

MRS. ALLAN. *(Rising and smiling broadly)* I must get back to Mr. Allan. Tell that Anne-girl not to forget us. We've invited all of her friends. And of course both you and Matthew. The party wouldn't be complete without you.

MATTHEW. *(Rising)* I'll show you out, Mrs. Allan.

MRS. ALLAN. *(As she crosses up stage)* Thanks. Goodbye, Marilla. *(Exits C. to R., followed by MATTHEW. MARILLA crosses to R. door and looks off again, then crosses to C. as RACHEL enters R., dressed as in previous Scene.)*

RACHEL. *(As she enters, eagerly)* Where's Anne?

MARILLA. *(Shrugging her shoulders; tartly)* How should I know? But I can tell you that I'm going to see that she stays home more after this.

RACHEL. *(Crossing to chair R. of table R.C. and sitting)* She's finally got over her peeve at me for buying them ten acres. *(MATTHEW enters C. from R.; goes to rocker L.C. and sits.)*

MARILLA. Matthew never has told me what he wanted that money for. *(Crosses up to R. of MATTHEW and regards him inquiringly.)*

MATTHEW. *(Nervously)* Why—er—I— *(As though suddenly inspired)* Yes, sir-ee, everybody in Avonlea says that our Anne's the smartest girl hereabouts. She does all my figurin' for me an' helps me considerable in runnin' the farm. She put over one deal for me that was a corker.

ANNE. *(Outside of R. door)* Matthew! Marilla! Where are you? *(MARILLA comes down C. as ANNE rushes in R. breathlessly. ANNE is attired in a lovely white frock of organdy or chiffon, the sleeves of which are wide and puffed. The same white shoes and stockings that she wore in previous Scene. All trace of freckles are removed. Her hair is curled and piled high on her head and held in place with a band of white flowers in the front that adds to her radiant loveliness.)*

MARILLA. *(Stands C., facing ANNE, her hands on her hips, a stern expression on her face)* Well, it's about time you were coming home, young lady. I thought you'd forgotten where you live.

ANNE. *(Rushing over to* R. *of* MARILLA *and smiling at her warmly)* Oh, please don't be cross with me this evening, Marilla dear. I'm so happy I can hardly breathe. Mr. Barry has been addressing me as Lady Cordelia all evening. I'm just dazzled inside. And Gil—I mean, a certain boy I know told Diana that—but never mind that now. *(Crossing up to* R. *of* MATTHEW*)* Matthew, I'm sorry to have to inform you that you left the milk pails outside of the barn and the barn door is open. (MARILLA *crosses down to sofa and sits.)*

MATTHEW. *(Rising)* In that case I'd better go out and 'tend to things. *(Placing a hand on* ANNE'S *arm)* My, but you look grand, Anne.

MARILLA. *(Stiffly)* That will do, Matthew. Anne is spoiled enough as it is.

MATTHEW. *(As he crosses to* R.*)* Reckon a little more spoiling ain't a-going to hurt her none. *(He exits.* ANNE *crosses to stand table in extreme* R. *corner and picks up the family album from off of same, then comes down to chair* R. *of table* R.C. *and sits, opening the album and starting to look through it.)*

RACHEL. Well, Anne, how does it feel to be growed up an' everythin'?

ANNE. *(Gravely)* Why, it just overwhelms me with the thought that there's so little time left in which to exercise my imagination, Rachel. My destiny is growing nearer every day.

MARILLA. *(Tartly)* I don't know what your destiny has to do with it, Anne.

ANNE. *(Earnestly)* Oh, but it has, Marilla. I can't make up my mind as to whether or not I want to be a trained nurse and go around rescuing people and saving them from death. Of course, that would be very romantic. But Diana thinks that if I studied hard to become an *inferior* decorator I'd have more scope for my imagination. I— *(Pauses suddenly, her eyes glued to a picture in the album; enthusiastically)* Oh, what a handsome boy! Every time I see him he just looks more beautiful. (MARILLA *rises and rushes to* L. *of* ANNE.) You know, Marilla, it's the picture that says "I. Mills" under it.

MARILLA. *(Snatching the book away from* ANNE*)* I've told you not to touch that album, haven't I, Anne? When are you going to stop disobeying me? *(Rushes up and exits* C. *to* L., *taking the album with her.)*

RACHEL. *(Tossing her head indignantly)* Well, I do declare, if that Marilla ain't the most impossible female I ever knew. I can't for the life o' me figger out what makes her so onery.

ANNE. *(Remonstrating)* You mustn't speak that way about Marilla, Rachel. It's most unfair. She's not responsible for what she says. You'd be twice as bad if you were suffering from the same ailment that she has.

RACHEL. *(Bewildered)* Huh? What's that? I never knew Marilla was sufferin' from anythin'?

ANNE. *(Gravely)* Oh, yes, indeed. It's a very serious ailment, too.

RACHEL. *(In puzzled tones)* It is? What's the matter o' her, Anne?

ANNE. Marilla is *frustrated!*

RACHEL. *(Agog with curiosity)* She is? What does that mean?

ANNE. *(With great solemnity)* Well, you see, Rachel, when Marilla was real young she met a boy and they fell madly in love with each other. He was just crazy about Marilla and they planned on getting married when they grew up and it was all so romantic that it just takes my breath away even to think about it. That was his picture in the old album and his name is written just under the picture, "I. Mills."

The "I" stands for Ivanhoe, so you can imagine how wonderful he was with a name like that.

RACHEL. You—you actually mean that Marilla had a beau?

ANNE. *(Nodding vigorously)* Of course. Marilla was so happy she went around singing all day long and their future looked bright indeed when suddenly a serpent reared its ugly head.

RACHEL. *(Bewildered)* Huh?

ANNE. *(Solemnly)* Marilla and her Ivanhoe quarrelled over some trifling matter that didn't amount to anything, though how she could squabble with anybody with such a distinguished name I'll never be able to figure out. But the fact remains that they parted and she was on the verge several times of admitting her mistake and asking him to come back but she was too proud to do it so finally when he thought it was hopeless Ivanhoe just picked up and departed and she's never seen him again. Isn't it too heart-breaking for words?

RACHEL. *(Amazed)* But why hasn't she ever told anybody about this?

ANNE. *(Gravely)* Oh, wild horses couldn't get her to mention his name. But though she wouldn't admit it she thinks of him all the time inwardly and that's why she's a trifle sour now and then and who can blame her when they just even think of Ivanhoe and how romantic he must have been? *(Rising)* It's all so sad I know I'm going to cry so please excuse me if I run out into the garden. *(Rushes to door R. and exits quickly. RACHEL sinks back on her chair, a baffled expression on her face. MARILLA enters C. from L. and comes down to L. of table R.C. She has discarded the album.)*

MARILLA. Where's Anne?

RACHEL. *(Rising)* She's out in the garden cryin over you.

MARILLA. *(Reluctantly)* Well, perhaps I was a bit too sharp with her. But—

RACHEL. *(Breaking in hastily)* Oh, that ain't why she's cryin'. It's because she says you're *flustered.*

MARILLA. *(Crossing to below sofa, bewildered)* I'm what?

RACHEL. *(Following her over to* R. *of her)* Marilla Cuthbert, I'd never o' believed it o' you—never!

MARILLA. *(Facing* RACHEL, *bewildered)* Never have believed what of me? Whatever are you talking about?

RACHEL. *(Knowingly)* Oh, you needn't try to hide it. I know all 'bout that Mills feller an' how you an' he was engaged an' how you fought with him an' he walked out on you an' never come back.

MARILLA. *(Aghast)* You—you—who told you?

RACHEL. *(Astonished)* Then it's true? Anne told me.

MARILLA. *(Stammering nervously)* But—but—how d-did she f-find out?

RACHEL. *(Triumphantly)* Then you did have a beau after all?

MARILLA. *(Beside herself with annoyance)* No—I mean *yes!* But I can't for the life of me understand how Anne knew about it. *(Rushes out* L.I. MATTHEW *enters* R. *carrying a newspaper in his hand. His manner shows that he is greatly upset.)*

MATTHEW. *(Coming to* R. *of* RACHELL; *tremblingly)* W-where's M-Marilla?

RACHEL. *(Turning to him anxiously)* What is it, Matthew? What's the matter?

MATTHEW. *(Warningly)* Now, remember, we mustn't tell Marilla a word about this.

RACHEL. *(Fearfully)* 'Bout what?

MATTHEW. *(Tremblingly)* I was so taken with Anne's school exercises this afternoon that I forgot to look at the evening paper. I just left it in the barn where I found it a few minutes ago. Look at these headlines. We're ruined, Rachel—ruined at our time of life. *(He hands her the paper, takes over to chair* R. *of table* R.C. *and sinks onto same.)*

RACHEL. *(Opening the paper and scanning it quickly; shrilly)* "Failure Of The Bank of Avonlea! Doors Are Closed As Depositors Lose Everything!"

MATTHEW. *(Weakly)* Every penny we had in the world was in that bank.

RACHEL. *(Tottering over to sofa and sinking onto same)* Us, too. Oh, whatever are we goin' to do now? *(DOORBELL jangles.)*

MATTHEW. *(Rising)* I wonder who that can be? Now remember, Rachel, not a word of this to Marilla. *(Crosses up and exits* C. *to* R. RACHEL *starts to sob loudly.)*

MARILLA. *(Enters quickly* L.1, *anxiously)* What are you crying for, Rachel? Has something happened to Anne? *(Takes up to* L. *of sofa.)*

RACHEL. *(Sobbing loudly)* No, it's worse than that. Our bank has failed an' we've lost everythin' we have an' you have, too.

MARILLA. *(Gasping) What?* (RACHEL *hands her the paper and she scans the headlines hastily.* MATTHEW *enters* C. *from* R., *followed by* GILBERT, *who is dressed much the same as in previous Scene. His necktie and shirt may be changed if so desired.)*

GILBERT. *(As he follows* MATTHEW *on; gravely)* I came over as soon as I could, sir. *(They come down* C., GILBERT R. *of* MATTHEW.)

MARILLA. *(Looking up from the paper; dazed)* Matthew, is this true? Was our money in this bank that failed?

MATTHEW. *(Darting an angry glance at* RACHEL*)* Didn't I tell you not to tell her, Rachel?

RACHEL. *(Sobbing)* Oh, an' just to think o' how we slaved for that money! We'll hafta sell the farm an' like as not we'll all starve to death.

MARILLA. *(Sinking onto sofa, L. of* RACHEL; *to* MATTHEW, *anxiously)* Does—does this mean we'll have to give up Green Gables, Matthew?

MATTHEW. *(Gravely)* I'm afraid so, Marilla. I don't care so much for myself. I'm old and not long for this world. But what's to become of you and Anne?

GILBERT. *(To* MATTHEW*)* That's what I came over to see you about, sir. It won't be necessary for you to give up Green Gables. You see, I have some money in my own name that was left me by Grandmother. The family have nothing to say about it. I want you to take it and use it to save Green Gables. I know what this place means to Anne.

MATTHEW. *(Taking* GILBERT'S *hand; deeply touched)* That's mighty fine of you, Gilbert—mighty fine. But of course we couldn't think of accepting such an offer. *(Lowers his head, crosses down R. to settee and sits.)*

MARILLA. *(Tearfully)* Oh, why did this have to happen to us?

RACHEL. *(Tearfully)* That's what I can't figger out. An' me with all them young 'uns. Oh, it's more than I can bear. *(Emits a series of loud sobs.)*

MARILLA. *(Shaking* RACHEL'S *arm savagely)* Oh, stop that crying. We all feel bad enough, I reckon.

ANNE. *(As she enters R.)* Where's Matthew? He's not in the barn and— *(Pauses at sight of* GILBERT *and turns to R. door.)*

MARILLA. *(Rising)* Anne, come here this instant. This is no time for foolishness. (GILBERT *crosses up and stands in arch, his back to the audience.* RACHEL *sobs loudly.)*

ANNE *(Crossing to* C.; *bewildered)* Why, what's happened? What is Rachel crying about?

RACHEL. *(Loud sobbing)* Reckon you'd cry, too, if you'd lost your money as we all have.

ANNE. *(Astonished)* What?

MATTHEW. *(Quietly)* It's true Anne. The bank, with our money in it, has failed.

ANNE. *(Hastily)* Which bank, Matthew?

MATTHEW. "The Bank of Avonlea." It closed its doors today.

ANNE. *(Calmly)* I'm not at all surprised. It's a wonder to me that it managed to stay open as long as it did.

MARILLA *and* RACHEL. *(Together, amazed)* What? (GILBERT *turns, listening intently.)*

ANNE. *(To* RACHEL *and* MARILLA*)* A short time ago Matthew insisted on placing his money in a joint account with my name as the other half. Then he gave me a power of attorney to sign his name to deeds and things.

. MATTHEW. *(Rising; to* MARILLA, *apologetically)* You see, Marilla, Anne's got so that she takes care of all my bank business and does all my accounts for me. So I thought it was the right thing to do.

MARILLA. *(Jumping up quickly; angrily)* Matthew Cuthbert, you're a fool, trusting all that money to a young girl. I never heard of such a thing.

RACHEL. *(Sobbing)* Well, it don't matter now. The money's gone anyhow.

ANNE. *(Silencing her with a gesture)* Just a minute. Listen carefully now. The day after Matthew included my name in the account and gave me the power of attorney, I went to the bank and had a talk with the President. That man just wore me out with his stupidity. He didn't have even a spark of imagination.

MARILLA. *(Crossing to* L. *of* ANNE*)* What difference did that make?

ANNE. *(Smiling lightly)* Well, it made all the difference in the world to me. I wasn't going to allow Matthew's money to stay in any bank where the President didn't have any imagination, so I just transferred the account to another bank that is safe and sound and your money is intact—every penny of it.

MATTHEW. *(Rushing up to* R. *of* ANNE*)* Anne, is this true? Did you really do that?

ANNE. *(Nodding assent)* Of course. The money is in "The Grand National Bank" and the President of that bank has even more imagination than I have, so your money will never be lost.

MARILLA. *(Throwing her arms around* ANNE *and hugging her impulsively)* Oh, Anne, you blessed girl. You've saved us from ruin. Oh, whatever should we have done without you? *(Releasing* ANNE. *To* MATTHEW, *stonily)* There, you see, Matthew! And you were the one who wanted to adopt a boy. Reckon you're mighty glad now that Nancy Spencer made the mistake she did. *(Kisses* ANNE *on the cheek.)*

MATTHEW. *(Shaking his head wearily)* You're a wonder, Marilla. *(To* ANNE*)* You know how I feel about you, Anne. You've always known. *(Crosses down to settee* R. *and sits.)*

ANNE. *(Turning to* MARILLA *and smiling)* I know how Marilla feels, too. Only she never showed me until today. It's the first time you've ever kissed me, Marilla.

MARILLA. *(Brokenly)* I've always known that I loved you, Anne dear, but I never could let myself go until today. The day you kissed me for the first time I wanted to tell you how much I loved you but I just couldn't bring myself to do it. *(Kisses* ANNE *on the cheek affectionately)* I've just been an old fool.

RACHEL. *(Rising; loudly)* Well, of all things that ever were or will be. *Marilla's got mellow!* *(DOOR-BELL jangles.* GILBERT *exits* C. *to* R. MARILLA *crosses down* L. *and sits in armchair.)*

ANNE. *(Crossing to* R. *of sofa)* I never wanted Matthew to sell you the ten acres of land, Rachel.

But if you need some money we'll buy it back and let you make a small profit.

RACHEL. *(Astonished)* D'you really mean it, Anne?

ANNE. *(Nodding assent)* Of course. I'm sure Matthew won't oppose me. The land is worth a lot more than you paid for it, so we can afford to be generous.

RACHEL. *(Excitedly)* Well, that will save us and I'm sure we'll be able to keep the farm. I must go right over and tell my Tom. *(Rushes over to R. door, then turns and faces MARILLA)* If you'd ask *my* advice, which o' course you didn't, I'd tell you to let Anne take care o' all money matters from now on. *(Exits R.)*

MARILLA. *(Eagerly)* Anne, what did you mean by telling Rachel Lynde about my having had a beau and whoever told you about it?

ANNE. *(Stands direct C., looking at MARILLA)* You—you mean it was true?

MATTHEW. *(Before MARILLA has a chance to reply)* It's true, all right, but I didn't think anybody but us two knew it. Feller named Mills. Nice boy he was, too.

ANNE. *(Overjoyed)* It must be this lovely dress that has made everything come true. I just *imagined* about Marilla's romance. (GILBERT *enters C. from* R. *and pauses below* L. *end of arch as* FLORENCE REMSEN *enters C. from R., followed by* IRA MILLS. FLORENCE *wears a Summer traveling ensemble and is smartly groomed.* IRA *is a tall, powerfully built man in his early fifties, pompous and distinguished in appearance. His face is smooth shaven, his hair is liberally streaked with grey. Wears a dark business suit, stiff white shirt, stiff white collar, a conservative necktie. Carries a straw hat in his hand.)*

FLORENCE. *(Coming down to L. of ANNE and smiling warmly)* Anne, don't tell me you've forgotten me.

ANNE. *(Astonished)* Miss Florence! Oh, how grand to see you again! *(They embrace.* IRA *stands up with* GILBERT *and* R. *of him.* MARILLA *and* MATTHEW *rise quickly.)*

FLORENCE. *(Holding* ANNE *at arm's length)* How pretty you've grown. Where is the little girl who was always getting into scrapes?

ANNE. *(Shyly)* I still do. Ask Marilla. *(To* FLORENCE*)* I want you to meet my two dearest friends, Miss Florence. *(Nods toward* MARILLA*)* This is Marilla, who is an angel, and this is my Matthew—words fail me when it comes to describing Matthew *(Smiles at* MATTHEW.*)* And this is Miss Florence Remsen, who was so good to me when I was in the orphanage. (MATTHEW *and* MARILLA *acknowledge the introduction.)*

IRA. *(He comes down to* R. *of* ANNE*)* I think I'd better introduce myself, Miss. My name is Mills—I—

ANNE. *(Breaking in quickly)* You needn't tell me. I know. Your name is Ivanhoe and you and Marilla— *(Pauses and looks up at him earnestly)* Oh, I'm so delighted that you've come back for her.

MARILLA. *(Terribly embarrassed)* Anne, what are you saying?

IRA. *(Smiling at* MARILLA*)* It's all right, Marilla. I've been thinking of the old days during our entire trip here and making up my mind what I'd say to you. But first I must talk to this young lady. (FLORENCE *takes over* L. *to below sofa.* IRA *faces* ANNE*)* I'm sorry to have to inform you that my name isn't Ivanhoe—it's just plain Ira.

ANNE. *(Visibly disappointed)* Oh, what a pity! Still, I could imagine that Ira is romantic.

IRA. *(To* ANNE; *in kindly tones)* I don't aim to be romantic. I'm just a businessman who has struggled and worked hard to pile up a fortune. Recently I started a search to find my niece, my dead sister's daughter, a little girl named Anne Shirley. (EVERY-BODY *except* IRA *and* FLORENCE *register wide-eyed amazement.*)

ANNE. *(Gasping)* W-what?

IRA. Yes, you are my niece, Anne. Miss Remsen has all the proof. I made a trip to the orphanage at Hopeton, Miss Remsen told me you were here and kindly consented to accompany me to Green Gables. *(To* MARILLA*)* You can imagine how surprised I was when I learned that Anne was in your care, Marilla. It seems as though a special Providence has looked after Anne all these years.

ANNE. *(Dazed)* And you are my uncle—my own dear Mother's brother?

IRA. *(Smiling at* ANNE*)* That's right. And I've plenty of money, Anne. Enough to enable us to travel and for you to have a fine education.

MARILLA. *(Crossing up to* L. *of* ANNE; *tearfully)* Oh, Anne, you won't leave us now, will you? I just couldn't bear it—I just couldn't. It would be so lonely here without you.

MATTHEW. *(Thoughtfully)* Well, I dunno. We mustn't stand in Anne's way, Marilla.

MARILLA. *(To* MATTHEW; *irately)* Matthew Cuthbert, you keep still. A body can't expect a mere man to understand such things.

ANNE. *(Turning to* MARILLA *and placing an arm around her waist; comfortingly)* Dearest Marilla, I'd never leave you and Matthew for all the money in the world. You took me in when I was alone and friendless and now— Stop crying, dear, or you'll have me doing it too.

MARILLA. *(Loud and sobbing)* I can't stop. It's the first time in my life that I ever cried and I'm just beginning to see what a relief it is.

ANNE. *(To* IRA; *gravely)* I'm sorry, Ivanhoe—I mean Uncle Ira, but I want to stay with the two bosom friends whom I love so dearly. I couldn't be happy any place but here. *(Crosses down R. to MAT-THEW, who leans over and whispers in her ear.)*

IRA. Well, that's that. I can't say that I blame you, Anne, and I admire your loyalty. I'll see that you have an income for the rest of your life and the future Mrs. Mills will continue to watch over you. *(Crosses to MARILLA, grasps her arm and places it within his own.)*

MARILLA. *(Gasping)* Future Mrs. Mills? Do I know her?

IRA. *(Laughing)* Know her? You *are* her. Come along, Marilla. I suppose I'll have to propose to you all over again. You always used to love hearing me propose. *(Crosses to door R. with MARILLA)* You know, I'm beginning to feel young again.

MARILLA. *(Beaming at him)* Mercy days, so am I. The fellow who said that life begins at fifty—er—I mean thirty-five, certainly was right. (ALL *laugh heartily as* MARILLA *exits with* IRA. MATTHEW *whispers in* ANNE'S *ear again; she nods in response.)*

(WARN Curtain.)

MATTHEW. *(Crossing up to L. of FLORENCE)* Wouldn't you enjoy a nice, cold drink, Ma'am? *(Winks at her significantly.)*

FLORENCE. *(In a knowing manner)* Why, how could you have known that I was just about to ask for one? (MATTHEW *and* FLORENCE *exit* L.I.)

ANNE. *(Crossing up to direct C.)* Gilbert, I've been sorry for weeks that I didn't speak to you the day you rescued me. It was rude of me not to thank you. You saved my life.

GILBERT. *(Coming down to R. of ANNE)* Oh, that's all right, Anne. I was looking for something to do that afternoon to kill time. *(Grins broadly.)*

ANNE. *(Gravely)* Matthew just told me that you offered your money to save Green Gables. It was fine of you.

GILBERT. *(Eagerly)* Are we really going to be friends, after all these years?

ANNE. *(Shyly)* If you still want to be.

GILBERT. *(Smiling at her warmly)* You know I do. And some day—when we're both old enough—I mean—

ANNE. *(Breaking in quickly)* Isn't it wonderful about Marilla and Uncle Ira? I wonder how Matthew will take it? I wonder if he'll be pleased?

GILBERT. *(Imitating MATTHEW's slow drawl)* We-el, I dunno. Can't say that he will and I can't say that he won't. Can't say but what he might and I can't say but what he mightn't.

ANNE. *(Clapping her hands together delightedly)* Oh, Gilbert, we're going to have such fun playing together. I'm sure that you have just loads of imagination and that will make everything so conducive.

GILBERT. *(Eagerly)* Anne, can't you use your imagination and look ahead far enough to the time when you'll be Mrs.—er—Mrs.—when you'll have—

ANNE. *(Breaking in quickly)* I don't want to imagine anything more than I have now because I'm so happy. For I'm Anne of Green Gables and that's all I ever hope to be—it's all I ever want to be. (GILBERT *and she join hands and laugh happily as the Curtain falls slowly.)*

END OF PLAY

ANNE OF GREEN GABLES

LIST OF PROPERTIES

ACT ONE

SCENE I

Small table with three straight-backed chairs sur·
rounding it direct Center stage.
Low, flat bench against Left wall.
Four or five letters in sealed envelopes (MINNIE).
Glass crash off stage up Right.
A faded old-fashioned sailor hat (ANNE).

SCENE II

Soft carpet to cover the stage with a few rag rugs
over it.
Old-fashioned doorbell ring (the sort that jangles)
off stage Right.
Screen door in Center of Right wall.
Stand table covered with a doily near rear wall up
Right; an old family album on top of stand
table.
Whatnot filled with miscellaneous articles in extreme
upper Left corner.
Rocking chair near rear wall and Left of arch.
Built-in settee with a few cushions on it against
Right wall below screen door.
Armchair in extreme lower Left corner.

Round table with three old-fashioned chairs surrounding it, well down stage and Right of Center.

Real old sofa with a few cushions on it Left of Center; an overstuffed hassock just below sofa.

Antimacassars for the backs of the chairs.

Old-fashioned oil paintings in wooden boxes, framed family portraits, bric-a-brac ornaments to dress the stage at discretion of director.

Knitting and knitting needles (MARILLA).

Large purse and a parasol (RACHEL).

Large geranium plant (MARILLA).

Large handkerchief, wide-brimmed straw hat and a gold watch chain across his vest (MATTHEW).

Newspaper (MATTHEW).

Old-fashioned valise (ANNE).

Small bouquet of flowers—either real or artificial (ANNE).

ACT TWO

A slate, several school books, and a pen and pencil box, all strapped together (ANNE).

Handkerchief (ANNE).

A white lace collar, wrapped in paper and securely tied (MATTHEW).

A small pocket knife (MATTHEW).

A black shawl and an old-fashioned gold brooch (MARILLA).

A large tray that has three glasses of lemonade, three forks, three napkins, and three plates on it, with a good-sized piece of layer cake on each plate (ANNE).

ACT THREE

Newspaper for First Scene (MATTHEW).

Pencil and a pad of white foolscap paper (ANNE).

Large dress box, unwrapped and tied with cord, and containing a white dress that is not removed from box.

Lighted oil lamp on table Right of Center.

Another newspaper used in second scene (MATTHEW).

White dress, white shoes and stockings, white band of flowers for her hair (ANNE).

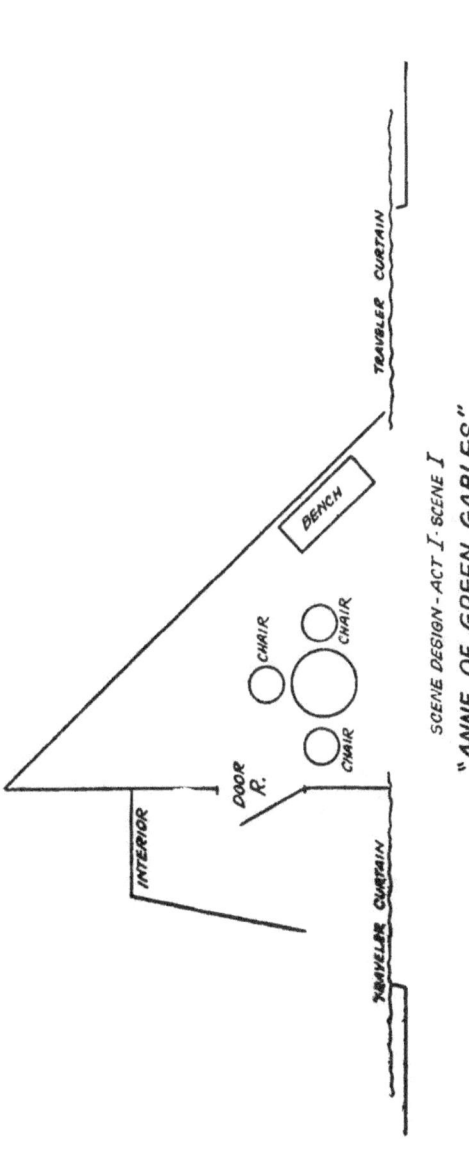

SCENE DESIGN - ACT I - SCENE I

"ANNE OF GREEN GABLES"

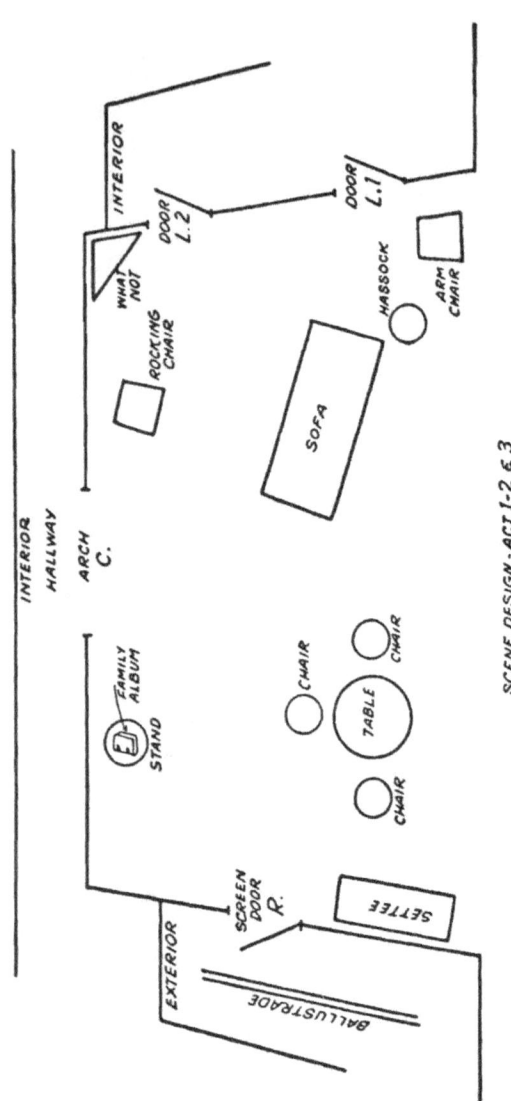

SCENE DESIGN - ACT 1-2 & 3
"ANNE OF GREEN GABLES"